THEY'LL
NEVER
Know

Dantes Involvement

BY O.Y. FLEMMING

They'll Never Know

Photograph By © Daxiao Productions
Cover Design By Bobbie Bohn

Dedication

This is for the thrill-seekers who live life in doses, and for the carefree that splurge.

~Yana

PROLOGUE

THE WINDY CITY

Dante

I've traveled substantially throughout my life, but I've never been to Chicago. I've had a few connecting flights, a layover or two, but nothing to bring me here to visit. I hear it's a beautiful city, but so is Miami. I know why it's called the windy city. I'm wearing a flat hat, and since I've stepped off of the plane into the open air, I've been holding on to it like no one's business. The wind is a force with no particular direction. It's an uncontained whirlwind on a course to nowhere. It will take some getting use to if my stay turns out to be longer than I intend it to be.

The taxis seem to be preoccupied on their own schedules, but rideshare is everywhere, and I plan on using them. The hotel where I have reservations at are located in the middle of downtown, or at least that's how their website describes it. It doesn't matter as long as I don't spend a fortune on getting around. I came here to accomplish one goal. It shouldn't take long at all, as long as Bryant cooperates. He's already made me come out of my way to see him. Even if Bryant is not aware of my visit his office in Minnesota shared information on his whereabouts, and any business matters should be directed to his temporary offices in Chicago. *How convenient.* I'm sure he'll be compliant. I'm also sure he doesn't want his hush money secret exposed. I've stretched that money as far as it could go, and I knew it would run out. I was hoping it would be later than sooner.

The ride share app on my phone opens as I tap the icon on the screen. It has identified my location so I type in the hotel name, and it appears in the drop down menu. Before I press request a ride a horn rattles my attention. An incredulous stare covers my face as the driver rolls the window down.

"Hey, you looking for a ride?"

"I am about to request a ride," my voice carries into the window of the Lexus. These drivers are doing well, apparently.

"C'mon I'll take you, my rider just cancelled."

"How will you get paid," I ask him yelling into the window

again.

"Just request a driver now, I'll accept it. Let me know when you do it. What's your name?"

"Dante," I deepen my bravado so he knows I mean business. I could take him if needed, as the thought of the rideshare serial killer enters my mind, I'm having second thoughts. My finger hovers over the request button, still reluctant about this guy. What driver shows up before they're requested? I tap the request button and watch the driver do the same. He pulls up closer to the curb to where I am not caring there is a line of cabs behind him trying to drive pass. I sling my duffle bag over my shoulder as his trunk opens.

"C'mon get in. We can beat rush hour if we hurry out of the airport. I can finally turn this app off and go home."

I know I'm a man, but this alarms me.

"I'm your last rider for the day?" My voiced deepens even more than normal.

"Yes sir, I live close to the hotel you're going to. A nightcap sounds good, but I've been out here for twelve hours. Sleep sounds better," he says.

"I see. That's cool." I put my bag in his trunk before getting in the back seat. The cool leather seat feels better than the airplane seat I was cramped in for an hour. The flight was short but the airplane was over booked so it was an uncomfortable experience sitting in the middle of two men equally the same size as me.

"Here for business or pleasure," the driver asks as he pulls off into the airport traffic.

"Business, definitely business." I fasten my seat belt, as the car starts to move. My body relaxes when my head hits the headrest.

"That's too bad, the car show is here. It's a really awesome event. It gets better each year."

"Oh yeah, maybe I can catch it before I leave." I say closing my eyes.

"How long," the driver asks. I understand these drivers are supposed to have a friendly disposition, but all I want is for him to be quiet.

"Excuse me?"

"How long will you be in town?"

"Hopefully my stay won't be long, I want to get back home."

"Somewhere warm, I'm guessing?"

I laugh.

"Not exactly, I live in Minnesota."

That answer got me an inquisitive look through his rearview mirror.

"I see," he says turning his attention back on the road.

"Hopefully after my meeting I can book flight somewhere warm."

He looks at me through the mirror again, he looks nervous. Which makes me nervous.

"Are you trying to get a job or something?"

"Something like that, I have acquaintances in business that owe me favors. I'm basically cashing in on them." I tell a half-truth, he doesn't need to know the glory details of my visit.

"Cool."

The driver became silent for the remainder of the drive. I noticed his entire demeanor changed when I mentioned where I am from. At the beginning of our drive he seemed relaxed. Now, his darting gaze tells me he's hiding something. His navigation system verifies that we a few minutes away from the hotel.

"So if I wanted to do something tonight is there anything close to the hotel?

"There are many bars around the hotel. I'm sure you can just walk around the corner and find something."

"Cool, I'll need something to occupy me over until my meeting. I don't like hotel bars they're overpriced."

"I hear that, if you want cheap, there's a bar north of the hotel about a five minute drive. Fifteen minutes if you walk. It's called BarCode. It's kind of a dive but they have kick ass shows, and the drinks are fucking awesome."

"I think BarCode sound good right now."

"They serve food too. The Buffalo wings are the truth I

might go there later. Take my card, text me, and I'll swing by to pick you up. No charge."

"Alright for sure," I tuck the card in my pocket without looking at it. The driver parks under the awning of the hotel. It's no wonder why my room is on the expensive side for one night.

"Talk about luxury," I say under my breath.

"You sure can pick them," the driver says ducking his head to look out of the window.

"Like I said if all goes well my stay will be short."

It feels good to stretch my legs again as I walk around to the back of the trunk. The ride was quick despite being in the back seat. Sometimes cab rides seem longer when riding in the back seat. Maybe it's all in my mind.

"Thanks man, I'll hit you up later after I attend my meeting," I extend my hand to the driver before entering the hotel.

"For sure, you'll like the joint. I'll swing through when you're ready."

"Alright," I say shaking his hand. This dude could not of

grown up in another country. He has no Asian accent whatsoever.

The hotel is definitely posh. It's just like Bryant to stay in a hotel like this. He's so arrogant his towels are probably those special moisturized towels given to the rich. There are a few people getting checked in, and I can't help but notice all of the representatives are men, *Okay, so I was going to flirt my way into a free night's stay.* Unless one of them likes men I will be paying full price, indefinitely. I laugh to myself at how far I would go to manipulate my way into what I want.

"You can step down sir," one of the hotel representatives says as the current customer walks away.

'Hi."

"Hi, how can I help you today? Do you have a reservation, or are you booking now? If so, I need your photo identification and a credit card."

The front desk clerk takes my card and I.D., not looking up until he gives me a room key as he rattles off the policy. I'm only half listening because my mind won't allow me to focus on anything that could potentially cost me more money than I have for his trip. What is that old saying? Never put all your eggs in the same basket. In my case the basket is small, and I'm eleven short from a dozen.

"Do you have any questions sir?"

"No, thank you."

"Your room number is on the key sleeve, enjoy your stay." He says friendlier than he first appeared to be. He smiles as I put the key in my back pocket. I glanced at the number three sticking out from the fold that holds the key.

"Have a good one," I tell him, as I walk away to find the elevators. I'm glad I'm only on the third floor, anything higher I'd lose my fucking mind if I were to look out of the window. The elevator is empty when the doors open, I rest my body against one side when I step on. The mirrored doors make me look older than I really am. The life I've made for myself isn't privileged like Bryant and his friends. Some might say I envy him, and the life he created for himself. Well I do, and my envy brought me here. The elevator doors open to a cart full of linens, and towels coming right at me.

"Yo, I'm right here!"

A five-foot wide-eyed female jumps from behind the cart, startled holding her chest. I'm taken aback buy her appearance, she's naturally beautiful. I can't help but notice her big brown eyes. They are not perfect. I bet people think they are weirdly shaped. *They are.* Right at the corner they hold a point. She's exotic in an islander type of way. My body stiffens a little at the sight of her. I think I'm in need of some air. The force of the cart feels like I've been thrown off a cliff, and the pressure from the fall has sucked the air from my lungs.

"I am so sorry, I just started today. My trainer left me on this floor with very little instructions," her voice is shaky and low.

"No worries, sweetheart. I'll get out of your way, this is my floor."

"Again, I'm sorry. I hope I didn't hurt you," she says

I'm sure you could.

"No, I'm fine. I've been hit by worst," I wink as I walk pass.

I dig into back pocket to retrieve my room key, as I do I notice from the corner of my eye the five foot beauty peeking around the cart from where she pushed it. The smile that she is wearing matches mine as the elevator doors close.

The room is as posh as the lobby. What made me book a room in the same hotel as Bryant Morgan? He can afford this this. I can't. No sense in me fretting over it now it's done. Bryant must have seen my email by now. He knows what time I arrived all I have to do now is wait. He told his personal assistant to give me his location when I asked her to give him a call while I waited at his office back home. He's expecting me. He's probably not expecting the reason I've been trying to contact him. I wonder if he's told Bria I am visiting? She moved here last year, and according to her social page she's getting married. How did she put it? 'After an ever so long engagement.' I never thought the feisty woman could be tamed. Surely her fiancé knows about her problem, or likes that kind of stuff. An abusive relationship was never my thing. Being on either side of abuse is not the kind of relationship I want. Love, respect, and a lifelong companionship are what I want to give, and receive. Outside of oral of course.

The very first time Bria laid her hands on me, she had gotten so mad she punched me in the chest. I didn't show her I was in pain at first, but it was a delayed reaction. Her little fist knocked the wind out of me. I doubled over gasping for air. She told me to man up, and that she hit like a girl. I wanted to call her bullshit, but I was trying to catch my breath. The second time is still funny to me, because that girl had some weird habits. I brought her food on a Styrofoam plate; needless to say she doesn't like Styrofoam very much. I earned a second-degree burn from the contents on the plate, and a handprint that resembled someone waving on my face. I vaguely remember the year and a half I spent as her punching bag. I knew she had a problem, she was also verbally abusive, most of the time I laughed at her outbursts. They were so random that I threatened to leave her if she didn't get help. Bria was so clever she finessed a full credit for enrolling in a program for anger management.

I was proud of her for taking responsibilities for her actions. I was honored that she valued our relationship. Bryant hadn't cared one way or another. He dangled me bait to leave his best friend alone, to transfer to another college, and never come back. I took the money, and I left like he wanted. I didn't believe the lie he told. I know he didn't sleep with Bria back then. I knew they were close, but they never fucked. I knew. I just saw dollar signs.

My room overlooks the front of the hotel. The patrons seem so rushed as they run in and out of establishments on the Mag mile. This city scream high-maintenance, what city calls a mile of shopping and entertainment, magnificent mile? Chicago. It's cold as polar bear balls here, just like Minnesota's cold weather. I don't understand why Bria chose a crappy weather state.

In the reflection of the window my phone lights the room. There's an email message from Bryant. He will be back at the hotel in thirty minutes. He didn't say anything else. He's so vague, his email didn't lead me to believe he wanted to know what I wanted to see him about. I can't help but to keep thinking about what he thinks about me contacting him. After he stated that I should never come back, I never intended to. Looking up from the phone and out into the city's sky, I've never seen such an amazing skyline. I've seen pictures, but to actually witness it, is serene.

The hotel is buzzing with some sort of convention. There always seems to be something going on every time I stay in hotels, people are everywhere. I should probably go back to my room, rather than sit here and people watch them until Bryant arrives. I'll stay because most of my time is taken, any time wasted will kill my plan. I'd rather meet him when he arrives, so I'll have the upper hand.

"Fancy to find you here Mr. Williams," Bryant says from behind me. He doesn't look up as I stand to greet him. He's pre-occupied typing on his phone. When he's done he lifts his head, and stares at me as if I'm annoying him. Extending my hand, I step around the couch and try greeting him again. The bastard is still as arrogant as I remember. He looks down at my hand before he shakes it.

"Let's talk in my office, there's too much going on out here," he says walking pass me. I nod and proceed to follow. Bryant leads me through the first floor of the hotel where the offices are. He unlocks a door to a suite, and pushes the door open wider, extending his arm for me to go in first.

"Damn man, you really know how to lived it up."

"Not really, as a shareholder and the man responsible for saving this place they treat me well."

This is the point I want to ask him to hook a brother up, because my room isn't cheap. Shit this entire trip wasn't cheap. The man in me won't though. I came here for a reason, not to come off like a weak ass man looking for a handout. However, what I'm about to spring on him would probably be considered the same thing. *A handout.* This way will be dirty, but I've been known to get dirty, grimy even.

"So Dante what brings you to Chicago? My personal assistant said that your visit is considered to be urgent. Why is your visit considered to be urgent," he asks leaning on his desk that sits outside the living room. I haven't moved since I walked in. Reluctance stiffens my body. I'm having second thoughts about going through with this. I regain my sovereignty because I need to control this situation, and not let Bryant see any weaknesses. My hands are sweaty inside my pockets. I held on to this piece of paper since it fell into my lap. I slowly pull it out, and hold it before extending my hand to Bryant. He takes it, while looking at me suspiciously. Bryant reads the paper far longer than I expected him to. He stares at it as if he can't believe what's on it. Our roles have switched. His body has stiffened, as my resolve is now calm. I have the upper hand. There's no way for him to take it away from me. I can tell by his breathing he is not happy about what's on that paper. Bryant slowly lifts his head, the tribulation in his eyes tells me he's battling what to do next. He doesn't say anything, he doesn't move, or flinch. I allow my right hand to fall by my side, as my left stays balled into a fist in my dress pants. Bryant still hasn't said anything, and I don't think he is going to. I clear my throat to get his attention as he is staring off. Bryant's expression is blank I can't read him. I do know I want to get out of here now that I've dropped a bomb.

"Contact me with your with your thoughts to make this go away."

CHAPTER 1

FRIDAY NIGHT

Dante

I enter my room for the second time today, and immediately I feel a pang of anxiety. Closing my eyes, I inhale through my nose, and let the breath out though my mouth. I can't believe I did it. The elevator is filled with patrons of the hotel it's a good thing too. Being around people kept my anxiety in check. I definitely need a drink after that intense ten-minute meeting. If Bryant gives in, I'm set for life. If he doesn't I will find another way. *I need a drink fast.* I can't have it here in the hotel. Bad enough I'm staying here under the same roof as Bryant. I don't want to indulge in a fifteen-dollar for glass of ice, neat, and run into him again. The rideshare driver gave me his card in case I needed to get a drink. I pull it from my shirt pocket, and flip it on the printed side. The back is just badass black. It's an actually color called badass black.

It's a distinguish hue.

Anton Tae is what the driver card reads. I text him right away so I can get the hell out of here. Bryant is too close for comfort. He might try and make me disappear. I heard him and Bria are good with that.

Hey. You still down for drinks?

D.

A few seconds pass, and my phone dings.

Cool, on my way.

I remember him mentioning he is only a few minutes away. That will give me just enough time to dress for the bar. I'm not looking for anything tonight other than a drink. My phone rings from a Minnesota area code I don't recognize. I let my finger hover over the accept button longer than I intend to. I know it's Bryant, I would make him wait, but this is not a game. I tap accept.

"Yeah."

"What's my timeline, and who else knows?"

My mind won't function as quickly as I want it. I only

planned on being here for a day or two. Tomorrow being Saturday, the banks close early. I have to take this into consideration, but Monday is too long to wait.

"Sunday, I leave Sunday."

"What the fuck man? You're putting me in a tight position."

I don't say anything because I don't give a fuck about his position. With what I know, he can lose everything.

"Who else," he says reminding me that I didn't answer him the first time.

"No one."

"Let's keep it that way," he says with what sounds like through gritted teeth. "I'll contact you in the morning with the transaction transfer number."

"Yup," I say hanging up before he says anything else.

I've never been intimidated by Bryant, physically I can take him. His financial status is more intimidating than anything he does. Some time has passed when I realize my messages on my phone.

I'm out front.

I waste no time leaving the room, I need to clear my head to process what's about to happen. I can go off the grid and no one would notice. I have no doubt in my mind that this will change my life. It was too easy, I know Bryant he won't give in to my demand without gaining something for himself. Only this time I'm not with Bria. All scenarios cross my mind as I take the elevator to the lobby. Anton is occupied on his phone when I exit the hotel. I walk around to the passenger side to get in.

"My bad man, I was on the phone when your text came in."

"It's cool, I haven't been out here long. Valet gave me a little static, but it's cool."

"This bar any good?"

"It's a dive, but like I said, the drinks are worth the buck. The entertainment is good most of the time. What keeps me going back is the hot bartender. I keep asking her out, but I think she's into females," he shrugs.

I laugh at his candidness. "Why do you think that?"

"I never see her with a guy, she flirts with everyone, but never anything serious beyond working for her tips."

"There's your answer right there," I tell him.

"What, give her bigger tips?"

"That, and maybe she's private."

"Her privates are nice," Anton says smiling.

"That's wrong man," I say laughing at his joke.

The bar is busy, there's a band on the stage performing when we arrive. We take a booth on the floor where the band is. I like the fact that The place is different there are two bars on the main floor. It's not crowded at either of them. There's a different atmosphere in here. The view isn't bad either, mainly because the female bartender who is taking our drink order has very nice breasts. They're just the right size not to be phony, but they make you think that they are. The little five-foot hotel attendant had a nice set of breasts, and from what I saw her hips were wide enough to have a nice ass too. I wish I had more conversation with her. She was working and I was on a mission.

"What are you having handsome," the bartender asks me. She's gorgeous and not a lesbian. I know this because her nipples are hard, and it's not cold in here. She's either aroused, or this is her natural reaction. Either way, she's not hiding it.

"I'll have a whiskey neat."

"What about you," she asks Anton.

"You know, I'll have Tequila and lemonade, and keep them coming."

"You want to open a tab handsome?"

"Yeah, why not.

The bartender smirks at Anton's choice of drink.

"You think my drink is feminine, don't you?"

"No, but you can tell a lot about a man by his drink choice," she says still smiling.

"Women say that a lot about men. Our hand size; our shoe size; how we eat a peach. These things tell you ladies a lot about men," he says sounding annoyed. The bartender bursts out in laughter.

"What so funny," Anton asks her.

"A tequila and lemonade tells me that you want something smooth that will keep you buzzed, but not slap you in the morning," she says turning to walk away. She turns back with her lips curled up. "Oh and your drink also says your an emotional drinker who doesn't like the burn going down."

I'm the one who burst out laughing this time. Anton eyebrows furrow as I cut my laugh short.

"That's foul man, I didn't bring you out for drinks for you to laugh at her jokes about me. That's cold."

"Man, it was funny. You're wrong about her though. She's definitely not a lesbian. She might be a little rough around her edges, but into women she is not."

"How can you tell what she's into? I know she's a ball buster," he says still looking pissed.

"You can't be mad," I say still half laughing.

"No, I just like tequila and lemonade. It is smooth, it doesn't give me a headache as long as the lemonade is made with agave and not sugar."

"Man you sound like an ingredient encyclopedia."

"I know a lot of shit about nothing, sometimes it's good to know shit. It helps with figuring people out, mainly women," he says rubbing his chin.

"Are you like a professor or some shit outside of driving for that ride share company?"

"No, I have to lay low for a while. Driving is the only thing that I could do until things blow over."

Who in the fuck am I associating myself with? It's bad enough I know about Bryant's illegal shit. I don't want to know why the taxi driver has to lay low. If this doesn't work out with Bryant, I'm going to jail for extortion. Walking back to the hotel sounds like a plan so I don't get into any other shit. The bartender comes back with our drinks her breasts look even bigger now that she's closer. She shakes her head because she caught me looking.

"What does my drink say about me gorgeous," I ask just to get her to talk, but I would like to know what she actually thinks because women never really talk to me about shit like this. I haven't had many relationships after Bria, well none of them serious enough to mention. Bria is a triple threat, beautiful, smart, and driven. Her fiancé is a lucky man.

"You're a man's man. Whiskey neat says you sugarcoat nothing, but you don't want any trouble either. You avoid casualties, but you don't mind being the cause of some of them." Her body language is confident as she expounds on her theory of me. I lean back in the booth sliding my glass back and forth with one finger, allowing her words to marinate. Finally, I take a whiff of my whiskey. I lift the glass to my lips while staring at the bartender. The taste is very woodsy, my tongue tingles from the flavor.

"This is aged very well," I say lifting the glass into the light, inspecting its color.

"Yea, it's considered our house whiskey, the owner owns a bit of the oak staves."

"Kentucky?"

"Yea, how did you know," she asks with her hands on her hips. She acts as if she's interested in what I know about whiskey. I know a lot, the dad I knew dealt with spirits all my life until he died while I attended college. He never stopped talking, or teaching me about what he did for a living.

"Shit, he owns spirits in Kentucky? That's like MM's bourbon, right," Anton asks.

"Sure is," she confirms.

"Nice," Anton says nodding.

"I would love to sit and talk to you guys, but I have other less interesting customers, and a lazy co-worker to tend to. Let me know if you guys need anything else. I'm Neenah by the way."

"Thank you Neenah," I say with my glass lifted. She walks away to take someone else's order.

Anton pays his tab after a couple of hours. I didn't hesitate to pay mine after my second whiskey neat. They are cheap, and I wanted them to stay that way.

"Are you cool to drive man?"

"Yeah I'm cool. I'm going to the restroom, and we can go."

"Nah, I'm going to walk back to the hotel. I need to clear my head, and I need a little fresh air."

"Man this is Chicago, you let me know if you breathe some fresh air," he says giving me a pound. I've never met a more down to earth Asian guy; he amazes me with his personality. His knowledge of things in general is interesting to listen to.

"I'll catch up with you tomorrow," I tell him as I put on my jacket. I left Neenah a nice tip since my drinks were less than I intended to spend.

"Alright D, I'll catch you," he says heading toward the restrooms.

"You're leaving soon handsome."

I turn to find Neenah leaning forward on the bar cleaning a glass.

"Yes ma'am, I have an early morning, and I might be flying out tomorrow."

"Awh, you going somewhere exciting," she asks with her

girls sitting high. The tight white shirt is very revealing, but I try to ignore them.

"If Minnesota is exciting then, yeah."

She turns her nose up, "what's in Minnesota?"

I turn my head as two men arguing on the other side of the bar distract me. One looks suspicious, and the other seems nervous like he doesn't want to be here.

"Home," I answer looking back at her.

"I knew someone like you couldn't be from Chicago."

"Wow, someone like me. What does that mean?'

"You just don't seem like a Chicagoan, you have a different kind of swagger, that's all."

"As long as I have swag is all that matters."

She laughs, I find it kind of cute that she's flirting, but she's not my type.

"Well listen, if you're ever back in Chicago make sure you come back. We love out-of-towners. We'll treat you well," she says moving to the outside of the bar.

"Come on, give me a hug."

I extend my arms to hug her tight body. It feels good. She may not be my type, but my body says she is. We end our hug, and I walk out into the cold night air. It feels great, I hope my body numbs by the time I make it to the hotel. Traffic is still the same at one in the morning as it is at one in the afternoon. I make it back to the hotel quicker than it took Anton to drive to the bar. The bourbon I drank made me come to my senses. I thought about what Anton said about laying low. I didn't care much to ask him what he meant. I just knew I didn't want to get caught up in anyone's business I don't plan on helping.

The front desk attendant waves at me as I pass her. I don't want to come off as rude, so I wave back. The elevator can't get here fast enough. I haven't had any rest since I got off the plane this afternoon. I just want a shower and to go to sleep. The elevator door seems like they are opening in slow motion. I know I'm not that drunk, but when they do, the hotel attendant who ran me over with her cart earlier is leaning backwards on the elevator wall. Her eyes are closed until I step in. She's startled, and tries to hurry out of the elevator. She waves her hand between the doors as they are closing, but it's too late she's going up with me.

"Shit, I can't win today," she says in a low tone, which seems like she's hiding an accent. She raises her head looking up at the ceiling. The mirror shows her me, looking back at her. She slowly lowers her head, as do I, mirroring her actions as we lock eyes staring at each other through the elevator doors. I don't remember pressing my floor button when I got in, but somehow the doors open to the third floor.

"Are you sure," I ask her pushing away from the wall. I stand behind her, almost flush to her short frame. She's tense at first, as I intertwine my fingers through hers. Whatever she's holding in she lets it out on a smooth exhale. I move as close as I can be to her with our clothes on. My intentions are to get her to walk, but my dick is hard making it difficult for me to. She knows I'm aroused by this small display of affection. Our fingers are still laced together when the elevator doors close again. She lets her head fall back just under my chest. Neither of us is saying anything. Neither of us has moved. I've noticed the elevator has reached the fifteenth floor. The hotel has twenty-six floors, eleven more floors to go before either of us has to make a decision. She has relaxed a bit more, comfortable even as her fingers remain laced between mine but firmer now. I can imagine what kind of day she had after the cart incident. Right now at this moment, we stand here, silently expressing everything we carried on our shoulders today. When we exit, we will leave it all here. I let out a breath I didn't know I was holding until now. Maybe, subconsciously I don't want the elevator to go down, and exhaling is the acknowledgement that we've reached the last floor before we do.

It's like we are moving in unison, we both focus on the floors counting down. The seventeenth floor is where the elevator stopped, and my heart races as she tries to step away from me. I tighten my grip on our joined hands, and close the small gap she created before the doors open. A couple gets on and she leans her head against me again. The gesture is small but it gives me a sense of calmness. I expected her to get off the elevator earlier, but she is hesitant. I wonder will she go with me now. The elevator passes the tenth floor as we find each other in the mirrored doors again. Her eyes are sad, before I read relief in them. What made her this way, so suddenly? Am I too forward with this random act of affection? I lean my head forward, taking a deep breath to inhale her hair. It smells of something citrus, or maybe it's the chemicals she used to clean. Whatever it is, my body likes it. We've passed the third floor, and I don't want to let go. She feels right, fitted into me like we were made for each other. These last two floors feels like the end, when the doors open the couple leaves the elevator and our hands untwine. She takes a step forward, the distance is so small but I feel so empty. She doesn't look back as she gets off the elevator this time. I want to go after her, I want to take what's weighing heavy on her, and make it end. Although she doesn't look back she doesn't walk any further, but it's too late as the doors close, and takes us to different places.

CHAPTER 2

SATURDAY

Dante

The sun peeks through the drapes in that annoying way where one ray of light rests on my face. Every move I make into the darkness leaves me restless. As exhausted I was last night, I didn't sleep as long I would have liked. I can't stop thinking about her, about her eyes. I can't stop thinking about how she held on to me. I can't stop thinking about how she felt nestled into me. She needed something last night, something I could have given her only temporary. The elevator ride could not have been enough. Did it satisfy what she craved? Did I calm her mood? I know the act only made me want more, it makes me want the unknown.

I've been staring at the clock longer than two hours now, or at least it feels like it. There are four hours until I hear from Bryant. He has to be at the bank by now. Reality is kicking in as I lay on my back thinking about our brief meeting. He had the entire night to think things over. He could change his mind from what we agreed upon. As much as I don't want to leave this room until he calls, it's best that I do. Otherwise my thoughts will be my demise. The hotel has a weight room that I can work off the frustration. The burn will take my mind away from reality.

The gym isn't crowded, which is good. I don't need any distractions from what I want to accomplish. I find a corner to stretch in before I start lifting. I take my workouts serious especially when it comes to weight lifting. It can be dangerous without a spotter, and from the looks of my options I better play it safe.

After forty-five minutes my body needs a break. There's a water bar here, it's a bit overrated, but a good idea. I've never seen so many flavors of water. Tap is good enough for me. I grew up drinking it, and it hasn't killed me yet. There are a few more people working out on the machines, I didn't want to be here when it became busy. I grab a towel before heading back to my room. I didn't bring my cell down, and now I'm anxious to get back to check my messages. I don't even bother taking the elevator, there were so many people waiting. I decide to take the stairs to the third floor. It may have been a short work out, but the aftermath is the same. The last thing I want to do is offend anyone with the smell of sweat. At a fast pace I walk across the lobby to take the stairs. I only made it half way before I saw her. She is pre-occupied on her phone to notice me. I want her to notice me without drawing attention to myself. As I slow my walk I spot Bryant behind her, which is easy considering he stands two feet over her. He sees me right away as he nods in my direction. I walk a few feet, enough to be out of sight to my mystery girl, but for Bryant to see me. I'm staring past him when he approaches. He follows my stare to a group of people in matching t-shirts, who replaced the space where she was standing. I want Bryant to fulfill his deal so I can leave. I don't want him to think I'm here for any other reason other than to get paid.

"You have a minute? You look like you ran a few miles," he

comments on my disheveled appearance.

"Yeah, I do."

We walk back across the lobby to where his suite is. He lets us both in, and I take a seat on the chair. Bryant sits on the couch aside of me with his face in hands. The frustration that he shows extends to my mood. I stroke the top of my head a few times, still not looking up to acknowledge his demeanor.

"Look this information, –" he pauses. "D, man this is serious. How the fuck did you find this out?"

I still my hand from smoothing down my waves. I can't believe his question. "Does it matter?"

"It does, this is my life we're talking about. If you got it so easily, it makes me wonder who else knows? Who else will come after me?"

I finally look up, but Bryant doesn't.

"So what are you saying? Is this happening or what? I don't need to be here for this shit to hit media." I say standing from my chair. Bryant stands from the couch with his arms at his side. The rise and fall of his chest tells me he's defensive just like I am.

"How do I know you won't come for me, again?"

"Trust me I won't." I say staring him in the eye. Bryant isn't a small guy, and I'm sure he can hold his own. I'm not a small guy either, and never have I been intimidated about Bryant.

"But you did."

"Different circumstances B, different circumstances."

We were cool in college. I guess we had a common denominator keeping us in check. Bria's not mine anymore, and it looks like she didn't give Bryant a chance.

"What's different D," he asks stepping closer with both hands lifted at his side.

My mind says *money*. "Who you are, and who you claim to be?"

Bryant shifts his stance. He thinks about what I just said, as he looks in the air. "Who I claim to be?"

"B, you did it. You did this shit." I gesture my finger in a circle. "How I found out doesn't even matter. You're at a disadvantage? I'm at a disadvantage because I do know, and the amount to make it go away means nothing to you." Bryant steps to me. We are less than a foot apart, both adjusting our jawline.

"My life," he grits out.

I stare at him without blinking. I know how much Bryant is worth, he doesn't give a shit about losing money. If he did, he wouldn't have a career in corporate takeover. He paid me ten thousand dollars to stop seeing Bria before we were twenty-one. The money isn't the problem for him, how I obtained the information is. He's an arrogant asshole, who needs to know actions causes reactions.

I can hear the grinding of his teeth. "The money takes seventy-two hours to deposit into your account. I better not ever see you again." He breaks the intense eye contact, and opens the door. I'm sensing this is my queue to leave, but before I do I stop to shake Bryant's hand. His head slowly moves in the direction to where my hand is extended. It's only a gesture to show there's no animosity between is. The look on Bryant's face says there's more than animosity in the air. I don't give a shit, men like Bryant needs a reality check every once in a while.

"Hey it could be worse," I say smugly as I walk out of his suite.

"Fuck you D," he spits.

I don't respond to his anger it would only lead us down a violent path, quickly followed by jail time. *I'm good.* I walk back through the lobby to take the stairs to my room. I'm sure I'll offend people on the elevator with the way I smell. I take them two at a time with adrenaline racing through me. The walk down the hall to my room feels like a victory lap, with every stride taken it's been worth it.

I pace in my room as my thoughts takes over my mind. I am an over thinker and my own worse enemy. Every second that passes a new scenario strikes me. *Is this really happening? Will Bryant have me arrested for extortion? Is this considered extortion due to the nature of circumstances? Am I guilty by association?* I definitely need to check out of this hotel before Bryant figures out

I'm just as guilty as he is.

The cold water from the shower helped me stay focus on what I have to do. I don't want to relax yet. I want to know when the smoke clears, I can, without worry. I really don't want this agreement to turn into shit. I move fast placing my things in my duffel bag when my hand brushes across a folded document. The folded document that landed me here. The thing is, I don't know where it came from. It just showed up at my house one day. It was in my mailbox, in a sealed envelope with no return address or anything. I held on to this information for two months before I decided to do something with it. Bryant built his wealth off of a lie no one saw coming, but I'm the man to pull the blinders off.

After I scan the room for anything I might have missed, I sit on the bed. Adrenaline is still flowing through me strong. I'm not sure if it's because I know all of my money problems will be solved in seventy-two hours, or all the trouble I can possibly be in.

Bryant

The one motherfucker who I would never suspect to come for me, did. And what he has on me the devil would flinch. Dante doesn't want my soul though. He wants my money. Might as well be my fucking soul. Everything I work for is on the line, but he thinks it's priceless to me. What I do by bringing companies back to life is a gift that you can't measure that with a price. Dante doesn't understand that though, I don't think he gives a fuck. He thinks with his newly found revelation of information he can break me. The cocky motherfucker followed me to Chicago to extort a lot of money from me. He has a price, and it's not cheap. Although it wouldn't put a dent in my account, it would surely raise questions to my investors. I've made my financial statements public to show trust. If I make them private now it would send a red flag to certain shareholders who I'd rather not alarm. The fucked up part about it is that I have to give it to him, but how can I benefit from it?

I have one opportunity to make this right, or get rid of Dante for good. Either way the stakes are high, he's smart. He knows what this situation means. This will open the door for a full

on investigation of all my businesses. It is a mistake I made that

can send a domino effect crashing down to my world. I must have

been blind not to see this shit coming. My career has been good

not to think otherwise. There's always a proverbial phrase that

you look back on when shit hits the fan that reminds me of this

very instant. Mine has to be; *he who pays the piper calls the tune.* I

opened the door when I paid Dante off the first two times. The

second time wasn't to him directly, and this is why you reap what

you sow. This won't go away until Dante does, but I'll be damned if

I pay for it, again.

I can't trust him not to come back. I wonder why he is doing

this? Is he having money problems? I can give him a job. It'll raise

some concern given his college major wasn't in business, but

would it eliminate him from trying to extort more money from

me? I could keep him close so that I know his next moves. Dante

won't go for it, he's had his hand in a wealthy pot, and knows what

it's worth. How can I sell this to shareholders to accept Dante on as an advisor, or something? I have to think of something to avoid giving him anything with that many zeroes attached to it. I should have informed Bria when Dante reached out to me, but she doesn't need to know about this before her wedding. She, and I haven't been the same since I found out I was one of her male escorts. Something else I never saw coming, or anything after that night. Our lives will never be the same because of the secrets kept, secrets, which destroyed what we had.

I don't know why I'm ignoring the bigger picture. Maybe it's because all of my hard work will diminish if I don't go along with Dantes plan. If I do, I'll still stand the chance to lose a significant amount of clients. I rebuilt a brand on my name. My father hadn't reached his success this early on in his career as I did. My father was a fool with his success when he obtained it. He got involved with shit I paid for later. My father has been in the dark for a long time regarding my capabilities. I stayed ten steps ahead of him at all times. I didn't inherit his business I saved it and made it mine. He could never accomplish what I have with failing companies. He knows it, and he continues to stay away for those reasons. My father is smart in other ways that are beneficial to him. My mother calls him a smart fool. I never knew what that meant until I became older. He's made mistakes, some he didn't even know about. I've cleaned up after my father so many times before I was twenty-one I knew what not to do personally, and professionally. Most importantly I knew how to get out of it. In this business you have to know when to cut your losses. A simple know how won't cut it. Impulses and following trends will only get you so far. Most importantly you have to separate the owners with their companies. They become emotionally attached and make decisions based off of their emotions, which makes for bad business. I suggest owners to give me full disclosure of all financial statements, and plan strategically from any findings. It's overwhelming at times, but not to the point where I need to bring on another set of eyes. I thought when I hired Mike it would be a mistake, but it works for the company. He has brought on companies that we saved early on within their start. If offering

Dante a job will make this all go away I'm all for it. I don't think a job is what he wants, and it's damn sure not a job working beside me.

CHAPTER 3

SUNDAY

Dante

I woke up to the alarm from the bedside table ringing in my ear. I knew I would need it after the night I had. After my workout I made sure all of my things were in order, so that I could leave without anything slowing me down. I'm glad this will all be over tomorrow. I can go back to Minnesota to live the best life I can live. I don't have any plans after I receive the money. It will change my financial status, and that will change the outlook I have on my life. My phone rings from the table. I wasn't thinking to screen my calls before I answered it. I didn't think I had to until the voice on the other end became clear.

"Hello," Bryant's voice is raspy like he has just woken up.

"Yeah B, what's up?"

"Are you still here in the hotel?"

I don't answer right away, because I should have checked

out last night.

"I am, why?"

"Can you meet me in thirty minutes in my office?"

"Is there a problem," I ask anxiously.

"No, there's not a problem. Should there be a problem?"

"You called me." I say, now getting out of bed. *I should have checked out last night.*

"Just be in my office in thirty." There is silence on the other end, which can only mean that Bryant has hung up before I can protest. This can't be good, why the fuck does he want to meet me? I place my duffel bag by the door to prepare to leave. After I meet with Bryant there's no purpose of me staying in this windy ass town. I've almost lost a few hats since I've been here. I put on clothes before I head into the bathroom to brush my teeth. As I look in the mirror I realize that I can't check out until the money is deposited in my account. I didn't anticipate being here longer than today, but I knew I'd have the money by now.

I don't bother waiting the full thirty minutes before I head to Bryant's office. He's on the phone when I open the door. Bryant looks down at his watch, with his brows drawn together he signals for me to sit. I shake my head, and continue standing. Bryant ends his phone call with an annoyance on his face.

"You don't know how to tell time?"

"Yeah I do, and that I don't have."

"Don't have what," Bryant asks standing from his desk.

"Time."

"Are you in a rush?"

"To leave, yes. So can you tell me what this is about?"

"D, you have to have patience." Bryant looks at his cell phone then up at me.

"I'm all out of patience B, either we have an agreement or we don't. I just know I'm not staying in Chicago past today," I clench my teeth.

"I think you'd want to stay."

"Why is that, B?"

"I have a job for you."

"What?"

"Work for me. Here, in this hotel," Bryant says, and I believe he's serious. "I mean eventually you'll be working beside me. You know like partners."

I begin to shake my head, "no I don't know."

"You'll make at least half of what you're demanding the first six months I can guarantee."

"It's not a demand."

"It's damn sure not a favor, or a fucking loan." Bryant says defensively.

"It's more along the line of getting what is owed to me," I say plainly.

"You don't think being a part of my company is a good start?"

I let out a laugh at Bryant's candid gesture. He doesn't look amused that I'm not taking his suggestion seriously.

"I don't think that's a good idea. I appreciate the offer, but I'll take what I asked for."

"Listen, take a day or two to think about it, and make a decision then."

I try to keep myself calm, but this wasn't in my plans. I clench my fist at my sides so hard the inside of my hands will be bruised.

"Bryant I don't have a day or two. I'm going back to Minnesota tomorrow," my voice is steady but I know Bryant can hear my irritation.

"I didn't know you had anything to go back to Minnesota to."

That was a low blow, even for Bryant. He knows my mother passed away from an accidental drug overdose. Her neighbor found her in bed a day later. The coroner confirmed that she didn't suffer. The physician that wrote the prescription admitted to his mistake. There is a malpractice lawsuit that can take another three years aside from the two I've already waited through. Bryant is truly a ruthless son of a bitch, and I know, I met his mother on graduation night. He has an agenda, which seems like it doesn't include paying me anything.

"What's your angle? You want me close so you can get rid of me for good? Just deposit the money Bryant, and I'll be gone." I say impatiently.

"Are you having money issues," he asks with a concerned look on his face. I know it's an act, his smug ass doesn't mean well. Although the lawsuit would eliminate all my money issues, so can this payment from Bryant. I'm not going to volunteer that information. I'm not selfish, but Bryant can afford to lose a few millions.

"What?"

"Are you having money issues," he repeats himself. "It would be perfect to come work with me."

I push myself away from the wall that I'm leaning on

"Bryant I'm not interested in working with you, for you, or beside you. All I n—," I pause before finishing my statement. "The only thing you can do is let me know when my money hits the bank."

"Oh now it's your money?"

"Technicalities," I laugh out as I leave his office. I can't take Bryant's offer. I have a business plan of my own. Bryant thinks this is a game it's about time I let him know that I'm not playing.

Dante

The day isn't getting any better. When my mother passed away, I broke my lease to move into the house that she was renting. My landlord called complaining about my rent payment. She inappropriately suggested a different form of payment. I don't know what she's heard, but that's not my forte'. I guess the apple doesn't fall far from the tree. I've been mistaken for other men before, but man whore I am not. I should have given her Bryant's number. I heard he was Bria's main distinguished gentlemen, and didn't even know it. Bryant's pre-planned relationship funded Bria's escort services. She has always been smart, which is what attracted me to her. Bria's body didn't go unnoticed either. Her ass is what really caught my attention. She had bent over to grab her notebooks out of her car when I notice it, her. Someone else is reaping all the benefits of her, now. She had flaws, but they didn't make up the woman she was becoming. I shake my head to rid myself from thoughts of her. Being with Bria was bitter sweet. She was a breath of fresh air followed by the cough you get trying to inhale it all too fast. I wasn't in love with Bria, but I did care about her. She has a strong personality, which is what would have eventually ended us if Bryant hadn't interfered first. It was a blessing and a curse.

It's too late for breakfast, but too early to drink, and the way I'm feeling I need to eat before I start nursing this bottle I picked up in the hotel store. This fucking hotel is sucking me dry, and it doesn't feel good. By the time I get back to Minnesota I won't have anything left to enjoy if I stay here any longer. I need to get out of this hotel to clear my head. I've been sitting here since I came back from meeting with Bryant, trying to figure out what led me to take these actions. As always I never figure it out. I sit at the edge of the bed, and send off a text.

*Me: **Hey, what's a good restaurant in the area?***

Ellipsis appear.

*Tae: **There's an American grill two blocks east of the hotel. It's a steak, and potatoes type of place.***

I shoot off another quick text.

Me: **Thanks.**

Ellipsis appear again.

Tae: **You need a ride?**

Me: **Is it on the meter?**

Tae: **No meter**

Ellipsis

Tae: **Flat rate.**

Me: **Wow, seriously? I'll walk.**

Tae: **Lol, joking. I'll be there in ten.**

Me: **Cool.**

The restaurant is well worth my tab. I haven't had a steak like that since my mother was alive. She could cook any meat to perfection. She could smoke a pork chop like no one's business. It'll be three years since her death, and I really need to get back to Minnesota to visit her grave. Tae, and I are sitting in a booth when Bryant enters the restaurant with her. My. Her. My five-foot beauty is here with that grimy bastard. Just observing the way she's fidgeting tells me she's uncomfortable. Her constant darting eyes makes me wonder why she's with Bryant. He is her boss, but what is she doing with him? Just as I ask myself the question, it's as if the both of them could hear my thoughts. Two sets of eyes attentively lands on me. I don't avert, but instead stare right into her dark eyes. She doesn't look away, but Bryant does, following my path right to her. Bryant places his hands in his slacks as he walks toward our booth. His facial expression lets me know exactly how this conversation is about to play out. The small body woman trails behind him never taking her eyes off of me.

"Dante, I thought you were going back to Minnesota today," Bryant asks smugly. I lean back in the booth with both my arms spread across the backrest. I don't let on that I'm not in a rush to get back, but Bryant won't intimidate me in the presence of her.

"Nah, I'm waiting on a confirmation before I leave." I glance at my watch, then at Bryant. "A few hours or so," I callously comment before taking a sip of water. I glance at her standing beside him. I'm holding on to the connection we had in the elevator. She's not mine, but I feel possessive over her. I want to ask why she's with this asshole, but the man in me won't let me. Bryant notices that she's uncomfortable, which makes me uneasy about her standing here. We've never spoken, nor have we seen each other since the night in the elevator. Bryant raises an eyebrow when he notices Tae, who is occupied on his phone.

"Do I know you," Bryant points, asking Tae. For the short time I've known Tae he has seemed familiar, but I haven't been able to figured it out. He had a bit of paranoia when I first met him. Tae's lips are turned down as he shakes his head at Bryant's question.

"Are you sure you've never been to Minnesota? Bryant asks Tae again.

"I have not. People says everyone has a twin."

"Identical," Bryant says stuffing his hands back in his pocket.

"Aren't you being rude to your date," I ask Bryant, prying to get information.

"I am being rude," he says pulling her to his side. She looks regretful. "This is Sireen, she's a new employee who works for the hotel."

I nod her way, as she softly says hello.

"You should ditch this guy," I say pointing at Bryant. "I hear he's cheap and doesn't like to pay for services rendered." I smile at her, then at Bryant. He chuckles with his head lowered.

"You have a way with words D," Bryant says escorting her away from our table. She looks back in disbelief. I realized what I said wrong as they walked away. I didn't mean it in any way pertaining to her. Bryant knew what I meant, but I'm sure he's *not* going to explain it to her. There's a dreadful feeling building within me. I know it's because she's with him. I want to find her, and make sure she's not making a mistake. I want her to be the one person Bryant can't have. He can have anyone, except her. If I show interest in her, Bryant will use her as leverage. Bryant will try and play more games with my money if he thinks I want her. I want Sireen, very badly. At this point my patience is gone, and I need to remind Bryant what's at stake. Tae interrupts my thoughts.

"Let's get out of this place before anyone else claims they know me," he says, holding up his index finger to get the waitress's attention.

"You really should work on your poker face." I say placing my last forty dollars I have in cash on the table. "I have to use the restroom, I'll be back." Tae nods his head as I leave the booth.

The restroom is too cozy for a grill like this. Clean is one thing, but it's like a female made decisions on the décor. Why am I noticing this posh shit right now is beyond me, I expect it to smell of urine not Lavender potpourri. I leave the bathroom after washing my hands, as I make my way back to my booth a familiar voice calls out to me. My hands begin forming a fist, and my body is stilled because her presence always arouses my senses. I slowly turn to see her standing there. Her hair cropped at her neck, she's wearing a bright yellow coat that only the character Olivia Pope could pull off. It looks good on Bria though. She's as beautiful as I can remember her, naturally. It looks like she's picked up an extra two hundred and twenty five pounds. Either that or she has a bodyguard.

"Oh my God, it is you," she says standing only a few feet in front of me holding her purse, and cellphone. She looks hesitant, and the guy she's with looks like he's about to tear my head off. She takes a few steps and extends her arms. "It's good to see you, how have you been?"

"I'm good Bria, and you," I ask looking down at her, but quickly taking a glance behind her to acknowledge the now angry looking man by her side. He is definitely not her bodyguard. She pulls away from me quickly. Her right hand man is grinding his teeth I can tell the way his temples are pulsating, which leads me to believe that this is her soon-to-be husband.

He walks forward as Bria steps back. He possessively wraps his arm around her mid-section, splaying his hand over her stomach. She covers his hand with hers. My eyes dart to her stomach and back up to her face. Bria smiles a little, but quickly holds her finger to her lips indicating me to keep quiet. I nod confirming that I will. The question is, *who* will I tell?

"Dante, this my fiancé Cruz King." She looks up at Cruz who is still holding on to her. Cruz, this is an old friend, Dante Williams."

The man never took his eyes off of me until Bria lifted her hand to place on his face. It's like he's brought out of a trans with the touch of her hand. It would be a shame if I said I don't know what it's like to be affected by Bria's touch, because I do.

"Nice to meet you Cruz." I extend my hand as he steps forward extending his. Bria is standing between us with her hand intertwined with Cruz's.

"You too, how do you two know each other? Cruz asks looking at me, then down at Bria.

"We dated in college," Bria, and I both say in unison. Cruz gives Bria a side eye. She returns his gesture with a smile.

"You said you only dated one person in college," Cruz comments.

"I did," she says nodding her head once, "and this is him."

Cruz looks at me incredulously while Bria turns to him. I can tell she's mouthing something to him. He continues to stare at me, then down at her. She lifts herself onto her ball of her feet and kisses Cruz. He might be possessive, but she seems to know just what to do to put him into a better space. Cruz releases Bria, but kisses her forehead before he walks away. She smiles as she watches him walk away. Her eyes say she is proud, the way she smiles is indescribable. I can tell she loves him, she use to smile at me that way. She turns her attention back on me and the façade is gone.

Through gritted teeth she speaks to me without moving her lips. "What are you doing here?"

"I came to take care of business, I can't say the same for you, Bria."

"I'm meeting Bryant's here."

I can tell in her tone, it's not something she wants to do. I search her face because there's something wrong.

"Do I smell smoke in Bryant's world?"

She shakes her head in disbelief pulling out a card from her purse.

"Not here, not now. Bryant wants me to meet one of the hotel employees to see if she is a good candidate to be my assistant. My fucking workload has gotten out of hand. The temporary agency keeps sending me these young ass girls who are attached to their phones, or too high to comprehend what work is. In the end I find myself doing every damn thing anyway, and sending them home with no hope of returning."

"Look at you the business mogul you set out to be."

"Yeah, well the shit isn't easy. Got polices; compliances; sections; articles, or whatever the fuck is going on when lending financial help to these already fortune five-hundred companies."

I laugh, because the only thing that has changed is her dating status, it doesn't have me attached to it.

"What's so funny," she asks with her brows drawn together.

"You haven't changed, that mouth of yours is still—,"

"Inappropriate," she says interrupting my sentence.

"I was going to say filthy,"

She smiles deviously. "You *use* to like my filthy mouth."

I laugh again touching the bridge of my nose with her business card. This is the Bria I know. Always saying what's on her mind, cursing, and not caring who's around. It's also the Bria I know who is abusive, and as a man I can't let my guard down to her suggestive gestures. It doesn't stop me from saying what's on my mind though.

"I probably still would if you didn't have a six-two arm attachment claiming what's his"

"He loves me," she says quietly.

"Are you sure? Because it looks a bit like possessiveness."

She nods. "I'm use to being in control," she pauses. "With everything." Her eyes widen, and I can't help but letting out a loud laugh.

"It's not funny, you use to let me get away with everything."

I notice her body language, as she holds on to her phone

with both hands. She doesn't want to touch me, but I'm guessing if she hadn't been holding anything she would have given me one of her love taps by now.

"I did it to prevent you from being mad at me all the time. It didn't make me less of a man."

"I never said it did, Dante."

.She needs to stop saying my name, her voice is a soft melody that arouses me in a way her fiancé would not appreciate.

"You never said it didn't," I say, holding her card between my index and middle finger. She looks at it for a moment then back at me.

"I think we should talk, and like I said. Not here, not now. Call me so that we can meet somewhere. I don't think I'll be free until the middle of the week though. When will you be going back to Minnesota?"

"How did you know I *was* going back?"

"I just assumed you were." Bria focuses her attention on her phone as she becomes silent. Bria is a thoughtful woman, she may have had her problems but her heart is in the right place. I know what she's suggesting, this is why she'll always hold a special place in my heart.

"I will be leaving tomorrow to visit my mother's grave. If things go well, I won't be back."

She quickly looks up from her cellphone. "What things," she asks.

"Some business stuff," I say waving it off as if it's nothing.

"We have to talk before then Dante, but I have to go before I'm sent after." She turns a walks off.

"Bria."

She turns to face me.

"Congratulations." I say before walking away myself. I saw a little smile on her face as I did. I want nothing but the best for her, even if it's not with me.

CHAPTER 4

SUNDAY EVENING

Dante

Tae is back at the hotel sitting in the corner when I return. He texted me to let me know he had an emergency so he left. I took some time to see the city. Chicago is a city that needs no introductions to its history. It is the distraction I needed to think. What possibly could Bria want with me? She's about to be happily married, there isn't anything I can do for her. I stand in front of Tae with both arms extended.

"What the hell, man. What was so important that it made you leave me in the restaurant with my blast from the past."

"I told you I had an emergency situation," Tae seems annoyed by my line of questioning. I raise an eyebrow at the evasive tone he's giving me.

"An emergency, which brought you here?"

"I dealt with it, then I came here to make sure you were cool."

"Why wouldn't I be," I ask. Tae's concern is suspicious. I'm a grown ass man who hasn't been looked after since I was twelve. My mom trusted me to stay home alone while she worked. I haven't had a male concerned for my well being, ever.

"I don't know, I thought you'd be pissed because I left."

"Nah man, I'm capable of getting around the city of Chicago. Thanks for the concern though." I give Tae a handshake as he stands.

"What are you doing tonight?"

"I'm not sure," I rub the stubble that has grown in on my jaw. "I need to check out of this place to stay somewhere cheaper," I tell Tae realizing that I have stayed longer than my bank account has allowed me.

"I have an extra room, if you need a place to crash until you need to leave."

"What will it cost me?

"Bro, it won't cost you anything. I just noticed every time you mention something it has a dollar sign attached to it. I figured you don't want to spend too much on this trip."

I rub the back of my neck to relieve the building stress I've been under since I got here.

"Damn, is it that obvious?"

"You've asked how much everything will cost you since I picked you up at the airport. Yeah, it's obvious as fuck. What's the deal?" Tae asks looking around. I mirror his actions, because of where I am. The lobby is too public to talk about anything if I wanted to, and I don't so I keep it simple.

"I had some business deals to close, every cent counts, so I'm careful with my money."

"You have to do shit, man. You can't live your life in doses. You have to nourish yourself with good shit. Sometimes the good shit means splurging, if you don't splurge every once in a while it can be depressing. Doses keeps you in restraints, it keeps you from being comfortable, happy even," Tae says simply.

"I don't think I live my life in doses, I think I live within my means."

"Do you?"

Tae locks hands with me for another handshake. "Think about it, I'll be around this area today. This ride sharing thing is where it's at." He winks as he nods.

"I'll think about."

"Okay, just remember what I said. Doses."

Tae leaves the hotel, as I notice Bryant standing in front with Sireen. I'll avoid the two until I don't have to anymore. Bryant looks in the direction of Tae and pauses before he enters the hotel. Sireen isn't coming in she's looking at her phone when I notice Tae pulling up. She gets in without any hesitation she must have requested a cab. Tae pulls away from the curb into traffic. Bryant notices me as he passes the lobby. He stops in front of me. The look on his face says this conversation is not going to be pleasant.

"You are beginning to piss me off."

"Why, are just figuring out that I'm not going anywhere

until you give me what you owe me?"

He laughs, rubbing his chin with his free hand, the other is in his pocket. This arrogant motherfucker is always standing like he's posing for a photo shoot in a fashion magazine.

"No, you're like a fucking gnat that won't go away, until you die." His eyes are cold as he stares at me. The thing about Bryant is that he's never experienced a real ass whooping. I believe I'm just the man to hand it to him.

"You're too damn old to be a bully Bryant, but you aren't to old to get your ass kicked. By noon tomorrow you'll see how very much alive I am." I pat him on his shoulder as I pass him. He doesn't move from the spot where I left him, as I make my way back to my room. I have what he wants, and he has what I need. Neither of us can stand to lose anything at this point, but I need to get back to Minnesota before Wednesday. I prefer to know that I've received the deposit before I get home. The way Bryant is playing this whole situation I won't have it my way.

I can't stay here another day, but tonight is already billed so

I'll sleep here. I'll take Tae up on his offer after all.

I might as well take Tae's advice, to splurge a little, maybe in the hotel bar tonight. I don't feel like attending anything on the social scene so I guess it isn't splurging at all.

After a few whiskeys neat, I sit in the far corner of the bar. I watch people as they enter. Bryant sits slumped over at the end of the bar nursing on a bourbon. He looks as stressed as I feel. I make sure he doesn't notice me. I'm not in the mood for his bullshit tonight. He sits up when a small frame woman stands beside him. I can't make out who she is until the light from behind the bar radiates on an angle, revealing her to me. It's her, Sireen. Bryant pulls out a bar stool, she looks around before she sits. They don't see me, I prefer it stays that way. Getting out of here is on my agenda now. I don't want to see Bryant all over her. I might lose my shit if I see any affection between the two. It's too late though. She smiled at something he said, it makes me furious to see her happy with that prick. *What's wrong with me?* Sireen smiled, the only thing I want to do is break Bryant's face. He has always made me angry even back in college. The only reason I've never kicked his ass was because of Bria, she would always be the voice of reason for the both of us. Bryant's secret doesn't change anything either, knowing what I know now I still don't like him. Actually I dislike him even more. He's a privileged prick, who made sure information stayed hidden.

Sireen's current mood has an affect on me, which isn't normal. I should want to see her smile. I should want to see her happy, but I don't. Even knowing her name now, makes me angry. When she was the somber, mysterious, no name hotel worker I was sated. I can squeeze this glass of amber liquor that I'm holding until it bursts. The way she was in the elevator, how she leaned into me led me to believe she needed comfort. I was her comfort zone.

The bar is closing neither Bryant, or Sireen has moved. Unfortunately I haven't either because they are sitting at the entrance. I'm sure they'll spot me if I try to leave now. One of the waiter's gives me my tab. I hand him my card right away to avoid causing any attention to my dark corner. Bryant gets up from the

bar to help Sireen off of her bar stool. It is comical to see her sit

there despite her height. *I'm fucking drunk.* Bryant places his hand

in the small of her back as they leave the bar. I know I should give

myself time so they don't see me, but I want to make sure they go

separate ways. I move slowly out of my booth to make sure they

are not still standing where they can see me. Mainly because I've

had a few drinks too many, and where I'm from we're supposed to

be able to hold our liquor. Falling wouldn't look good on my GQ

status.

Standing isn't the problem, staying upright is though. I grab

ahold to the table using it to guide me to the next table until I make

it to the entrance of the bar. The waiter stops me before I leave to

give me my card. He's smiling so hard you'd think I'd gave him

more than a five dollar tip. I shove the receipt and card into my

jeans as I thank him for his service. *He didn't do shit.* Yeah, I'm

drunk as fuck, and I don't care. The hotel still has a few people

mingling in the lobby when I walk through to the get to the

elevator. Why people push the call button more than once is a mystery to me. Maybe they're drunk like I am, and think it'll come faster by the intense pressure they use when pushing the button twenty-three times in a single second. At least that's what it feels like. I only pushed it three times, and it's not here yet. When the elevator opens, Sireen is standing in the middle of it. The look on her face says I caught her off guard, with a side of 'you're a fucking idiot.' I step on directly in front of her, blocking Sireen from getting off. We are standing inches apart her head is lowered, while she seems unphased by our closeness, I don't know if it's an act. I can't focus with her being so close. Her scent is intoxicating me more than I already am. The elevator doors close, and unlike the last time the elevator doesn't move. We stand in silence for what it seems like forever. We begin to breathe together, both our chests rising and falling in unison. Anxiety is a creepy motherfucker, it sneaks up on you when you don't think it should. Instead of letting it take over me I control it with countering actions. I intertwine my fingers with hers like before, I reach behind me with the other to push all of the floor buttons so that it takes time to get to the last floor. Sireen stands in front of me unwilling to raise her head, but she didn't protest against what I was doing. I lower my forehead to hers closing my eyes. We ride to the top floor in silence with our foreheads still joined. When the door closes on the last floor I change my position. Still holding her hand I round her, moving closer so that our bodies know that we don't want to be anywhere else but together. Sireen lays her head on my chest as I lean against the elevator back wall. Our breaths flow together peacefully. I close my eyes on the remainder of the way down. She squeezes my hand when we stop on the lobby main floor. The doors open, but we don't bother to move. I push away from the wall with her weight still attached to me. I push the button to close the doors, but Sireen reaches out with her free hand, to stop them from closing. She hasn't let go of me yet, but shocks me as she looks back when she lets go. Her eyes hold that sadness that arouses me. It's my weakness for her, it's my beginning to her ending. I need this feeling from Sireen so that I can eliminate whatever it is. She doesn't say a word, and I know she feels my want for her. She stands there as I watch the doors close, too damn drunk to comprehend what the fuck I just did. I realize too late to go after her when I push the button to open the doors as many times that I can in a second, and the elevator begins to rise. *Fucking whiskey.*

Monday morning

Dante

My eyelids have been overworked they hold the weight to my headache, which is accompanied by stress. I don't know why I drank so much last night. It was definitely a mistake on my part. I left my dark shades back home, my eyes are not happy. This city has either a lot of shade, or constant ray of sun. Right now my hat is not protecting my face from any of that. Natural light radiates through the lobby near the checkout counter It's not helping that no one on the staff is utilizing the tinted shades. I can barely see the people around me with the amount of light entering into the room, so much that I didn't see Bryant rolling his luggage toward me. He doesn't greet me, but stands behind me as if we never met. The front desk attendant calls for me to step forward to check me out.

"Good morning sir, how can I help you," the bubbly clerk smiles. It's the fakest greeting I've ever seen. Bryant is behind me so I know it's an act. I noticed her whispering in her earpiece before she called me up. The staff probably gave her a heads up.

"I'm checking out this morning," I saying smiling back at her.

"Oh, okay, and was your stay pleasant?" She smiles even harder. I should screw with her and say that it wasn't, but I would rather just leave.

"It was fine, everything was fine."

"Okay, would you be willing to fill out a survey we are conducting about your stay?

She holds her head to the side while she bats her lashes. It's not working but I'll give her an *A* for effort.

"No, thank you," I tell her smiling, batting my eyelashes. She quickly changed her mood at my sarcasm.

"He's not that nice of a guy," Bryant says from behind me. I won't fall into his trap, so I ignore his comment. The attendant doesn't say anything, while she checks me out. She looks up from the screen she's working on, and the perplexed look on her face tells me something is wrong.

"Can I see the card you booked your room with?"

"Yeah, sure." I say handing her the card from my wallet.

"Ah, I see. Do you have another card you can use," she asks in empathetic tone.

"I don't, what's wrong with that card?"

"It has declined," she says softly.

"That's impossible, I only used the card a few times while I was here."

The attendant smiles, she shrugs her shoulders at my open admittance. I know I had enough money to cover the room at least for the weekend. I'm not sure what the fuck is going on, but I can feel Bryant watching from behind. He hasn't said anything but his presence just pisses me off in this situation.

"Can you try it again, but use debit this time."

"I tried both ways, I have to complete this transaction in order to go the next. Are you sure you don't have another card that you use until you get this one straight."

"I'm sorry I don't. I don't know why it is declining. It was fine last night at the bar."

"You were in the hotel's bar last night," she asks suspiciously looking back down at my card? I nod.

"Was it a problem with my card last night?"

"Just a second, please don't leave." She steps into the doorway of the front desk, and speaks into her ear bud. I can barely make out what she's saying but I did hear something about Jose having a big tipper at the bar. *Big tipper?* I gave the dude five damn dollars. Another attendant comes out to help the customers behind me.

"What's the problem," Bryant asks as he gives the attendant his card. He's seems genuinely concerned but I know there's sarcasm behind his question. After the awkward silence I simply respond without turning in his direction.

"There's a problem with my card."

He's quiet for a second, and I know the prick in Bryant is about to show his face.

"Rhonda," he calls for the attendant who is helping me. She

comes back to the front.

"Yes Mr. Morgan, how can I help you?"

"Go ahead and check him out as a courtesy of the hotel, and refund him for his charges."

"Yes sir, Mr. Morgan. So you heard what happened, then," she asks Bryant as she types quickly on the keyboard.

"No, I haven't."

The attendant must have over spoken, her face turns beat red at her blunder.

"Was it concerning my card," I ask her.

She nods not looking in the direction of either of us. Bryant turns his hand over, gesturing what happened without speaking. He's incredulous about it. I'm more embarrassed now for the attendant than I am for my card declining.

"It seems that Jose, your waiter doesn't speak, or read proper English. When he went to end your tab at the bar last night, he told Rachel that you were a nice big tipper. He was making a joke, but Rachel took it to be serious, and gave Jose a five-hundred dollar tip courtesy of your card." She has the most apologetic look on her face.

"Oh, so you can afford to pay for your room," Bryant nonchalantly says.

"There's the asshole I know," I say looking over my shoulder. The attendant eyes widen as she rushes to finish what she's doing.

"Rhonda it's okay, he's an old associate of mine. Glad to know your sense of humor hasn't changed D." Bryant pats me on the shoulder. It isn't friendly with the aggressive way his hand lands on my back a few times. I shoot him a side eye, indicating he's stepped over the line. Bryant lifts an eyebrow acknowledging his wrong.

"Ahh, I began to get worried," the attendant says looking up from the screen. "Okay you are all set, I have refunded your entire stay, as well as your entire bar tab."

"That wasn't really necessary, you could have refunded everything minus his five dollar tip." I say sarcastically because I can't resist. This was an inconvenience, and embarrassing. I could have easily caused a problem for Bryant's business, but I think I'm doing that already. I'm handed back my card just as Bryant is handed back his, we walk away side by side until he both come to a stop.

"You want to share a taxi to the airport and talk about the elephant in the room," he asks.

I shake my head. "There's no need to address what happens next Bryant. You have until noon, and looking at your current situation," I nod my head at his luggage. "You're running out of time, B." We turn mirroring each other. It's such an uncanny feeling that we both shift our feet so that we aren't matching each other's movements.

"Damn D, I just took care of your hotel stay."

"That I wouldn't have, if you would have answered my fucking calls. All of this could have been avoided."

Bryant shakes his head, and begins to walk out of the hotel. He doesn't look back or give me any notion that he will be depositing any money. It doesn't matter, because I will be getting

paid one way or another. By choice or force.

CHAPTER 5

Dante

I've been sitting in Tae's loft for two hours listening to him go on about women and plants. I have a strong urge to throw myself out of his sixth floor window.

"Tae is there anything you don't have a metaphor for?"

"Metaphors," he says as a matter fact.

I laugh at his answer, as he trims a plant that looks like it's been growing since I was born. I pull out Bria's card to give her a call, Tae stops what he's doing and gives me a curious look.

"What's up," I ask.

"How long have you known that chick who was in the restaurant?"

"Bria? How did you see her? I thought you were gone."

"I saw her as I was leaving. How long have you known her?"

"Since college, why?"

"She looks familiar, that's all."

I look at Tae suspiciously because he's been giving different vibes every time we hang out.

"What's your story? Bryant says you look familiar, now ironically you think Bria looks familiar. What's the deal? Are you a spy or something," I ask only half joking, because Tae doesn't know there's a connection between Bria, Bryant, and me. I remember the conversation we had the first night I arrived here. He said he had to lay low, lay low for what? I wait for a minute for his answer before I continue to make a call to Bria.

"Hello," she answers on the second ring.

"Hey what's up?"

"Hi Dante, are you still in town?"

"I am, do you think you'll have a little time for me?"

"Actually I will in about an hour. I'm meeting prospective hire at Maggiano's, you can meet me there if you'd like. I'll have some dessert or something," she says sounding distracted.

"Okay, I'll meet you there in an hour." The line is so quiet I think she's hung up.

"Dante," she says softly. I'm caught off guard by the sympathy in her voice, and I know where this is going.

"Bria don't, I'm fine. Everything's cool. I'll officially apologize to you when I see you, I'm not having this conversation over the phone Bree." Shit, I haven't called her that in years, although I haven't seen her either. I can imagine the look on her face as the afterthought of me calling her by her nickname stirs memories of her. The way she smiles ever so slightly when I pad my thumb over her cheek. The way she looks when I call her Bree. It all comes back, and I don't think it'll be a good idea to see her alone. With all the good memories, the not so good memories come to surface too. Those are the memories that I want to forget.

"I haven't heard that in years," she says matching my thoughts.

"It's a natural reaction, I said it before I even realized I was saying it," I tried recouping from my slip of the lip.

"It's fine Dante I haven't heard from you or Bryant in years, it is a nice memorable gesture."

"What does what's his name call you?"

"His name is Cruz, and it doesn't matter what he calls me."

"As long as he calls you, huh," I comment slyly.

"Are you meeting me for dessert or what," she asks deterring away from my remark.

"I'll be there."

"Okay, I'll see you then."

Our call ends and Tae is no longer staring at me, he has went back to trimming his plant.

"You never answered my question, Tae." I ask him. He stops what he's doing to look up.

"Nothing worth repeating, and sometimes."

I furrow my brows, thinking what kind of answer is that? Tae notices the look on my face and smirks. "I guess I have to kill you now," he says seriously, with a sardonic smile.

"The fuck?"

"You asked what my story is, I'm a spy," he still has a smirk on his face, which makes me unsure if he's joking. "Dante, man you are fucking easier than a ten dollar hooker on a Wednesday."

"That shit's not funny, man. I thought you were dead ass serious."

"I was."

It's quiet for a few seconds as we sit, staring at each other neither of us blinking. Tae seems oddly believable to actually be a spy in real life. He laughs as he stands from the couch.

"You're an asshole."

"You should feel right at home, then."

I shake my head in disbelief, "Don't tell anyone else that bullshit."

"Why, did you believe me?"

"I actually don't know what to believe coming from you." I stand from the small chair I've been sitting in. I'm twice the size of it. I don't even know why I sat in it, and for that long of a time. I rub my back from the ache I've developed from being in one position for so long. Tae opens a drawer on his end table, he hands me a card for a masseuse, and it has holes punched in it.

"It's a free massage I've earned I haven't been able to use, you can have it. It doesn't look like I'm going to have time to use it."

"Why wouldn't you have time, you going somewhere?"

A blank stare appears on Tae's face as he looks at me. He looks away as if I've just revealed the climax to his story.

"I'm not sure yet, he says as American as he can. I can distinguish a slight accent in his voice, which makes me understand, or at least I think I do.

"Awh man, they found you?"

He frowns at me, "who?"

"The government."

"The government, like I.N.S.?"

"Yeah, are you being deported?"

"Dude, no. I'm a United States Citizen, my parents gave birth to me here. Are you crazy." Tae says laughing.

"Well, shit. You're either being deported, recruited, or

arrested. Now that deportation is out of the equation. Are you being arrested for going A.W.O.L?"

"No," he half laughs at my guesses.

"I have a son I just found out about. His mother was in jail, and now is in a mental institution. I've had some time to come forth to claim responsibility. With doing so, it will open up another can of problems. He deserves at least one sane parent."

"Okay what's the problem, claim your son."

"It's not that easy, man," Tae shakes his head.

"It actually is, Tae. Unless you're an illegal alien go get your boy."

"I'm not, it's more complicated than that. My parents are always traveling, so they can't care for him. I don't know anything about her family to assume he'll be with them, I'm just screwed in the situation."

"I must be missing something Tae, he's your kid, why can't you take care of him?"

Tae doesn't say anything he just stares out of the loft's

window. Am I slow, or is this dude crazy for not just going to get his child? I don't have time for this type of shit this morning.

"Hey man, whatever it is, I'm sure it's not that bad. I'll text you when I'm ready to come back for the day. I don't want to interfere with your day, so I'll take my bag with me." I have to be cautious with this guy. He's revealing more strange shit by the day. I'd rather have my shit with me rather than leave them with him.

"I'll be around in the area today, when are you going back," he asks.

"Later today, or tomorrow. I'm not sure, but I'll know soon."

"Does it have anything to do with the guy from the restaurant?"

I don't answer him. Tae doesn't need to know anything about me but my name, and I don't want to know anything else about him than I already do.

"I'm going to meet my old friend for lunch, I'll let you know if I'm leaving in few hours." I'm sure he noticed I didn't answer his question, but I don't care. He's one less person I have to fuck with, here. When I leave I won't be returning.

When I arrive at the restaurant Bria is still meeting with her earlier appointment. It looks like she started dessert without me. I'm not sure why my adrenaline has spiked, as I get closer to her table. I know it's been a several years since I've seen Bria, but I've never had a feeling like this. It's more of an arousal than anxiety. As I near them Bria spots me, she waves me over. The other female's back is to me. Her head is familiar, as I stop at their table. Bria pulls out the chair besides her gesturing me to sit. As I pass the table to sit in the chair Bria suggested, I can fully see who her appointment is. It's Serene, she's just as shocked as I am. We both recover quickly before Bria notices. Before I sit I extended my hand, the hand she's familiar with. She slowly does the same. The adrenaline that I was feeling earlier now makes sense. It's definitely because of her. Her hand is warm just like the first time we met. Feeling her small hand firmly gripping mine sends sensations through me. It's funny because it hurts a little.

"I'm Dante Williams, nice to meet you."

"Hi, I'm Sireen McMillan. Nice to meet you as well," she says softy. Her voice is softer than I remember when she ran me over with the linen cart. It seems, a little abnormal now that I'm sober. Bria looks between the both of us, because we are still holding hands. Sireen pulls away first, with my hand still attached to hers. I finally release her hand without taking my eyes off of her. She holds confidence in her eyes, not the sadness I saw last night.

"You're obvious Dante," Bria says chuckling.

"Yeah?"

"Yes you are," Bria confirms.

"I don't care," I say briefly looking to Bria.

Bria, and Sireen both sit with their mouth agape. Sireen looks down at something in her lap, I'm assuming it's her phone.

"Ms. Watts, thank you for lunch. Thank you for your time, I really appreciate the opportunity. I look forward to next week," Sireen says with a slight accent.

"Sireen, I told you to call me Bria, it'll be easier because it's about to change anyway." Bria wiggles her ring finger. The size of her ring should be unmistakably that her last name is about to change.

"My apologies, Bria, thank you."

Sireen stands, as I do to show respect. Bria stands as well. The two shake hands before Sireen leaves the table. I watch her walk away, but I can't resist this urge anymore. I can't let her walk away without knowing what happened in the elevator wasn't just a random hook up. It wasn't even a real one. Bria is startled when I abruptly stand from the table.

"I'm sorry Bree, I'll be right back."

"Okay," she says nodding.

There isn't a rational explanation for my actions. My mind says leave her alone, but my gut says go after her. But nothing tells me what to do when she's standing in front of me, waiting. She doesn't face me, but I know she's waiting for me.

"You should have come for me last night," her voice barely audible.

"I—," I don't know how to respond, so I tell her the truth.

"I was too drunk to even know what was going on Sireen." I step forward to reach out to her.

"But yet you sat there in the bar and continued to drink."

"You knew I was there," I ask her with her back still turned to me.

"I watched you go in there before Bryant showed up, I sat there with him and listened to how big of a problem you were becoming to him as he drank himself stupid. You know the two of you are peas in a pod." *More than you know.* She still hasn't turned around to face me. I think this is becoming our thing.

"I don't care what he says about me, I came after you for you."

"You didn't come soon enough, Dante"

"What does that mean," I ask taking ahold of her arm, and gently turning her to face me.

"It doesn't matter, now."

"Why, what happened between last night, and now?" Her eyes tell a story that I don't want to hear. I take a step back away from her. I shake my head. She looks into my eyes, and I know. My look of disgust doesn't surprise her. If Bryant spoke ill about me last night it was only a matter of time he would convince her into his bed.

"I mean you did say, let's see, how did you put it? He doesn't like to pay for services rendered."

I can't be here with her any longer. Bryant's a manipulative prick who had to have noticed the way I looked at Sireen. If Bria caught on, I know Bryant knew how I reacted to her. I know he slept with her to get back at me. Getting away from Sireen seems like the best thing to do before I say something that will hurt the both of us.

"You go ahead and be happy with that," I say backing away from Sireen to go back into the restaurant. Something in the way she looks at me at this very moment has revealed more than the sadness she has kept underneath. Her eyes disclose sorry, while my gut realizes this is goodbye.

Bria is on her phone when I return to the table. She has a

gleam in her eyes as she speaks into the air. She points to her ear, and I see that she's wearing wireless ear buds. I sit in the chair across from her instead of the chair beside this time. She looks amused as she continues her conversation. Whatever is being said to her, it's making her blush. She's always sexy when she's easily embarrassed. Her fiancé has to be the one making Bria smile this way. Who else could be on the other end of the line? She ends her call, and turns her attention on me.

"So Dante, what was that all about," she asks gesturing to the seat Sireen once occupied.

"Nothing at all."

"What's that phone call all about," I joke with her.

"You are trying to change the subject," she says laughing.

"I'm sure whatever you and your fiancé were talking about is more interesting than what's *not* going on with me."

Bria wrinkles her nose. "That bad, huh," she asks.

"Nope, not bad at all. I dodged a bullet with that one," I point my thumb behind me.

"Were you interested in Sireen? She's really nice, soft spoken, like I was in college." Bria nods taking a bite of a pastry.

"Nah, I'm good. I don't need a wholesome girl," I say joking with Bria. I'm not joking though. I wanted Sireen because she possess a mysterious simplicity that I need. That simplicity holds me down, it brings calmness to the chaos in my life. I know we could have been good together, but just like chaotic shit in my world Bryant always seems to be rooted somewhere in the dirt.

"Wow,"

"That shocks you," I ask Bria.

"It does, because the Dante I once knew –,"

"Doesn't exist anymore," I rasped out.

Bria mouths *okay* as she sits up straight. I sit defensively because the more I visit here with her, I think about her perfect little life that she has made for herself. It pisses me off that Bryant ruined it for me. Even now, still rooted in my shit. My anger level has hit the roof now, and I'm not sure if I can contain it.

"Hey look, it is nice seeing you again Bree, I have to go. I just decided I'm flying back home tonight." I cover my hand with Bria's, and she hold on to me.

"Wait, I didn't get a chance to talk to you," she pouts her lips.

"That's isn't fair Bree."

"Please stay a little while Dante."

She knows I'll give in to her fucking pouty lips. *Sireen has pouty lips.*

"Okay, but what will your fiancé say."

"My husband isn't going to mind, he knows I'm here."

"Husband?"

"Yes, Cruz and I got married at the beginning of the year. Our schedules were crazy busy. One day we were having lunch in the building where the Justice of Peace is, he asked me to marry him. Again, right then. I said yes, no one knows but my parents and his wicked ass mother," she says rolling her eyes.

Bria hasn't released my hand, which has forced me to sit down, again.

"You don't like your in-law?"

"I do not. We have a little business history. It's a long story for another day."

"Wow, what the hell happened there?"

"Like I said it's too long. I said stay a while not a few days," she says laughing. "I'm sure someone will write a book about it, maybe a trilogy. The shit is crazy." Bria's still laughing, but somehow I think she's serious.

"How are things Bree, are you happy?"

"I really am. Cruz is a wonderful hothead. We keep each other balanced. He has had problems in the past as well as I did." She finally releases my hand to fan her teary eyes. "I asked you here to ask you a favor, not to talk about me and my husband," Bria pauses. "I've never heard myself say that until now."

"Are you just now realizing you have a husband?"

Bria stares pass me before she speaks. "I guess, yeah." We both burst out in laughter. I wipe tears away from my eyes, and cheeks. It felt good to laugh with her. We've always had the laughter in our relationship. It was second to the intimacy we shared. Thinking about it as she sits here with me feels wrong knowing she's married and about to have a family. It looks damn good on her though. She's glowing from her happiness, it radiates from her smile.

"Bree, you are something else."

She shrugs, still chuckling at her realization.

"What is it that you need for me to do?"

"I need for you to work for Bryant."

CHAPTER 6

Dante

Bria has dropped a bomb on me. Her husband picked her up about thirty minutes ago. I've moved to a small booth in the restaurant to think about her offer. Bria and Cruz's health clubs are expanding to more hotels to help the business. It seems that Bryant has took an interest in each hotel they've partnered with. Bria is worried that he is up to something. She's even more worried that Cruz will kill Bryant if he does anything to jeopardize their company. She want's me to work close to Bryant, and let her know what his plans are. She's willing to pay me a nice paycheck. It's nice and tempting, but I'm not getting involved with Bryant's and Cruz's pissing match. I'll let them sort out that shit on their own. I work for myself, no one else. It'll be the sweetest revenge on the both of them for what they put me through in college though. I had the choice of walking away without taking the money from

Bryant, but I was young and money was life back in college. Money is life now, but there's something about not having it that causes me to be angry. Sure, I could work for it. I can definitely go back to being an assistant manager for the publication company I've been at for the last few years. *I don't fuckin think so.* I am going to get what is owed to me. If I let Bryant get away with what he's done this time without it affecting him at all, I have failed my mother. If exposing him means I could lose everything I don't give a shit. I can't miss anything I've never had. He will not continue to further his success on a default created by him. I pull my cell phone from my jacket pocket. I've only looked at this piece of paper once since I've received it. It came with an explanation, and instructions where I could leak this information. I call the number on the bottom of the page. There's a long dead silence before the phone rings. When there's an answer the woman on the other end rattles off whose office I'm calling, along with the company's name. I didn't quite catch it, because she's laughing.

"I'm sorry, I didn't understand you," my deep voice must

have caught her attention. She makes a low guttural sound before she repeats herself slow and seductively.

"Good afternoon Trademark. You've reached Eve Waters office," she clears her throat again. This is Deneca speaking, can I help you in any way sir?" It sounds like she opened her mouth extra wide pronouncing each one of her words. I find it odd for a business to have someone this unprofessional answering the phone.

"Can you tell me if there is anyone who can help me? I might have a story they would be interested in."

"Yes, let me take your phone number. I'll have someone to call you back if we are interested."

"You don't even know what the story is."

"It doesn't matter, sir. If Mrs. Waters is interested she'll call you back."

"Can you please let her know she has an hour to call me back or I'll take it to someone else." The young lady on the other end takes an exaggerated breath, sucks her teeth, and sighs.

"Excuse me am I boring you," I ask her. "Let her know I have information on Bryant Morgan and the silence money," I read what's on the paper, rattled off my number, and end the call in the middle of the receptionist talking. I've made it up in my mind to fly back to Minnesota today. There's really no reason I should stay here any longer. Bryant flew out this morning, I'm sure. He has no knowledge of what I'm preparing to do. I check my account one last time before I request a car to the airport. I'll be back home in about two hours. Chicago is nice, but home is nicer. The confirmation of my request comes back, and thankfully it's not Tae. I wish that dude all the best, but I'll send him a text when I make it back home. I have a feeling building in the pit of my stomach as I walk out of the restaurant. Something unexpected happens when I feel this way. A short time passes when my phone vibrates. It's Bria. She must have made it home.

"Hello?"

"Hi Dante, I'm calling to apologize for dropping that on you so suddenly. I discussed it with Cruz on our ride home, and though he's very thankful he doesn't want to go through with it. Something else just came up we have to deal with before our wedding, and we really need closure with the tragic events that happened to us."

"Bree, are you okay." Her voice is broken like she's been crying.

"I am. I'm just happy that everything is coming together, finally. I don't have to live in fear," she says. She's full on crying, which is making it difficult for me to talk to her. It tugs at my gut to hear her this way. I can't be the man I use to be for her. *She's married now.*

"Is Cruz with you right now?"

"No, he's going down to the police station to identify the person who ran us down, and left us for dead."

"Holy shit Bree, I forgot about that. It was all over the news. I'm sorry I didn't reach out then. Cruz is the other victim," I asked.

"Yes, It damaged him the worse."

"You'd never know, your guy made a hell of a comeback."

"He did, he said he did it for me."

"I can understand that, I would have too."

The silence is awkward, but it's a good silence. Bria knows she's the one who got away.

"When did they catch him?"

"He turned himself in today."

"That's great for you two, you can finally close this chapter in your life," I say trying to give her a few encouraging words.

"Yeah, but I feel bad. He has a little boy who he hasn't met. The baby's mother is fucking psychotic she's locked up in a facility. That baby is going to grow up and resent both of them."

I remain silent because this is becoming all too familiar. Tae's story sounds a lot like he's the main character in Bria, and Cruz's story. I continue my silence while Bria goes on how her and Cruz can finally put this behind them. I'm getting another call while Bria is still talking.

"Hey Bree, hold on. I need to take this call."

"Okay, go ahead. I'll talk to you later, don't be a stranger," she says ending the call. *Her goodbye was longer than her conversation.*

"Hello," I say quickly into the phone. The caller hung up, it's dead. A series of text displays on my phone as the driver I requested pulls up.

"Going to the airport," he yells out of his window.

"Yes."

I get in with my duffel, there's no need to use the trunk. I'm not in the mood for anything extra right now. I tap my screen to see a text from Bryant. They keep coming in.

B: Are you out of your fucking mind?

I open the next one.

B: Do you know whom the hell you've tipped off?

They keep coming through, one more aggressive than the other.

B: She's the worst person to report anything to.

I laugh at his anger, he seems mad.

B: She was just beginning to leave me alone.

Seriously, who is this chick?

B: D, who the fuck gave you that information?

I don't know.

B: Answer me you fucking bastard child!

And I do.

D: A bit harsh don't you think?

The phone rings immediately.

"You rang," I say into the phone.

"What the fuck did you tell her?" The irritated tone in his voice displays more than anger. *I give zero fucks.*

"Hey B, how the hell are you?"

"Don't fucking play with me, D," he says through gritted teeth. I could barely make out what he said, but apparently, he thinks I'm fucking playing.

"This ain't no joke B. I told you what needed to be done. You didn't do it, so I made a phone call."

"What the fuck did you tell her?" I can hear Bryant on the other end grinding his teeth.

"I'm not telling you shit until you tell me about my deposit."
The phone is silent. I hear Bryant fumbling through what sounds like papers. He's talking to someone. The only thing I can make out is, 'make the funds available'. I do know my account number by heart, and those are it he's repeating to someone. He's confirming the time. He repeats two hours.

"D, the money will be there in two hours. Now what the fuck did you tell nosey ass Eve Waters?"

"I need to know why you fucked her, B?"

I've completely changed the subject.

"What? Fucked who," Bryant asks annoyed.

I want to know why couldn't he leave Sireen alone. She is the one thing I wanted more than his acknowledgement, and more than his money.

"What the fuck D? What are you talking about? I don't need to tell you whom I've fucked. I'm not the person who you need to keep tabs on, but that will be hard to do now wouldn't it?" That comment was low, even for Bryant. His reason for continuing to insult my mom is beyond me. He doesn't stop there though.

"Are you going to make it back to visit your dead mother's grave?"

Blood is piercing through my body so fast my head is spinning. When I get back to Minnesota I am going to deliver these hands to Bryant, personally.

"How long before my money deposits," my voice is so low and guttural I've shocked myself. I know I've put fear in Bryant because he hasn't responded. After ten seconds pass he speaks.

"It'll be two hours."

There is something in his voice that I can't distinguish. Bryant's not a pushover, but he sounds concerned. He thinks I've ousted

"Two hours is all you have. If it's not in my account, all you have will be mine."

I can faintly hear Bryant's growl on the other end before the line goes dead. Soon after my phone rings again, the number isn't a familiar one.

"Hello?"

"Hi, how are you? Are you the young man whom called me concerning a story," the woman on the other end says.

"This is Dante Williams, who is this?"

"I'm Eve Waters, Chief editor with Trademark media productions. My assistant stated that you might have information regarding a very prominent businessman." Eve Waters, and her assistant are very different. The two are like night, and day. Eve is a poised professional. Her assistant was unacceptably unprofessional. I can hear how confident she is. Her speech is articulate. It's not the way she speaks that turns me on. It's the tone of her voice that sends the signal from my brain straight to my dick. The way she speaks is confident, yet cautious at the same time. It's my body's wake up call. If she keeps talking I'm going to have to find a bathroom to relieve myself when I get into the airport.

"Yes, I do. You'll have to excuse my manners at this very moment. I'm on my way back home, and I've just arrived at the airport. May I call you when I land?"

"Yes you may, then maybe we can set up a meeting since you're on way back."

Judging from the number that I called, Eve lives in Illinois and I won't be coming back here.

"I apologize, I live in Minnesota. I won't be returning to Illinois."

"I'm sorry, did you say Minnesota," she asks.

"Yes ma'am."

"My husband's from Minnesota. He's a—,"

"My apologies, I need to check in and grab boarding tickets. I'll call you when I touch down. Thanks for returning my call," I quickly say to get off the phone. It's partially true. She doesn't need to know that I don't give fuck about her husband. That information ruined the fantasies I wanted to have about her. Listening to the way she spoke made me want to imagine how she'd sound when she moaned. How her lips looked, or if she kept them open when she moaned. Now, I don't give a shit. Her husband gets all of that.

"Yes, sure. Please make sure you call me back," she says curtly.

"Thanks, have a good day."

The airport is surprisingly slow. I got my boarding pass, and made it to the gate less than thirty minutes. There aren't many people going to Minnesota today. It's still early, so that can change. There are so many social media apps to keep me occupied before I fly out. Technology's progression scares me to the point that I have disabled my location on all of my devices. Trouble seems to find me all by itself, there's no need to help it. I open a text from Tae, I must have missed it when I was on the phone. It says, *'never take your freedom for granted, but take it in doses.'* The message makes me think about what he said about splurging. Freedom is a choice you have until you decide to do something to force you to give it up. I hope he's not the person who did that to Bria and Cruz. It would be a shame for his child to grow up without either of his parents. I can truly understand how he would feel.

The dad I knew died from alcoholism. He was a functioning

alcoholic, a great provider for my mother and me. He never raised his hand to either of us. My dad wasn't that kind of alcoholic. You know the type where alcoholism would turn a man into a demon. The same type you would read about, who would beat his wife and kids. My pops was a cool guy he harbored alcoholism, the disease. He raised me to survive, be respectful, and cognitive to all things. He had a style that I picked up on somehow. He was a down ass dude, who taught me to be my own man.

I can remember when I was ten, I came home pissed because one of my classmates was voted coolest boy in class. Nowhere in school house rock did this matter. It was something each class made up, to vote, classmates passed notes and voted with tick marks. Who ever accumulated the most was the winner. I won best dresser, and cutest boy. Back then it didn't take much to win cutest boy, and it helped that my dad bought me the best clothes I could have at that age. We didn't have uniforms back then unless we attended a private school. My pops told me never give up on something I wanted unless it wasn't good for me. He told me to pave my own way to become the person I wanted people to know I am. If I was the coolest boy in class, I should be that cool boy in class and own it. That next week, I won coolest boy in class, best dressed, and cutest boy. He told me if anything was mine I should hold on to it, never allow anyone take it away. If they did, regain it and claim it back. What my dad instilled in me, I've incorporated every lesson into my life. I was at school when my mother told me about his death. I was a junior in college, when I was interrupted from taking my finals. Thanks to my pops death, I aced all my finals. The college applied my last grade on each unit test as my final grades. *Thank you pops.*

My dad's death shook me, but my mom's death stilled my world. Although it was an accident I don't believe I truly recovered from it. It's been two years since she's been gone, and I still haven't grieved for her properly. My mother was my everything. After my dad died she told me he wasn't my biological father. It didn't matter because he is the only father I knew. They say when you're around someone so long you develop similar features. People use to tell my dad I looked just like him, he'd just smile. Both my parents are from interracial families so our family blended well. I've never met my biological father, and I don't think I want to. He made his decision on my life when he left my mother. Her death was sudden it took me a week to plan her memorial because she wasn't supposed to die from pneumonia. Feelings I've been holding on to suddenly hit me like a truck. I began to shake in the small seat attached to others in a row. Leaning forward I rest my head in my shaking hands to calm myself. This is what Tae's little boy is going to go through. He won't have anyone to care for him like real parents would. It's a shame he'll have to grow up without them. Instead he'll learn that one is mentally unstable, and the other committed a crime. It's not fair to him, and whoever raises him should know that what they teach him about his parents should be positive. No matter the situation. I continue to think about this entire weekend, how things went here, how things are going to end. I am going to need a vacation after all of this. I become calmer as I take a few deep breaths. The airline representative announces my flight with the departure time. I've been sitting here for quite some time not realizing the time I will arrive back home. All of my problems will be gone by the time I make it home. I'm not proud how I reached this point, but with every action there's a reaction. Bryant should have known better. He was depending on the dead not speaking. Someone knew what he did and knew whom to tell. I'm not proud of my actions, but I don't feel bad for him. He caused a lot of problems for the people I love, and now he will pay for it.

The young lady calls for the first group to board and I put on my headphones. The resonant bass of Cocoa Butter kisses by Chance The Rapper blares from them while we begin to walk onto the airplane. As I enter the hanger the lyrics are interrupted by a notification, but it doesn't catch my attention until it interrupts the rapper's lyrics again. I enter the plane, there's a single seat in the front row where the flight attendants are. I maneuver my duffel in the overhead carrier so I can move into the row quickly, out of the way of the others boarding. I tap my screen to see the notification that keeps interrupting the song. It's a notification from the bank.

Immediately I check my watch to verify the time. It's too early to

be the deposit that will change my life. The notification takes me

directly to the bank site for me to enter my username, and

password. My heart is pounding way too fast as blood rushes to

my head. I began to sweat as I wait for my phone to reveal my

account. When it does I can't fucking believe what my eyes are

witnessing. There is a message that says to contact the bank

immediately. I look around to see if anyone is watching me. I've

become paranoid suddenly, and I have to take a seat. I stare

straight ahead in disbelief. I managed to get what I deserve out of

Bryant and his silent money. I am fifty million dollars richer

because he never wanted me to be apart of that world. The dead

didn't speak, but someone very alive did.

CHAPTER 7

THREE WEEKS LATER

Dante

I haven't quit my job yet, because I need to pay taxes. It should be the last thing on my mind considering I don't have to work. I still can't believe I pulled it off without Bryant hunting me down. I would like to forget about everyone, and go where no one knows me. I've been seeing old classmates more often than usual. I understand that saying, 'more money more problems,' maybe it's me. All of a sudden I think everyone has a hidden agenda, when they're only saying hello. Bryant hasn't come after me, and it's not that I'm concerned, but it's been too quiet. I've gone back and forth with myself about giving the money back, and working with him. Needless to say I've talked myself out of it. I also keep telling myself this is what is owed to me.

A few people from work are meeting at the local bar. I agreed I would come this time. Usually I decline the offer because I didn't have the extra money to spend. This Friday night, I decided to relax a little. I parked away from the door so no one would notice I purchased a new truck. I'm still carrying paranoia around with me. I don't want anyone to ask me any questions. When I get into the bar half of my department is here, which makes me want to turn around and leave. I'm spotted before I change my mind. My counterpart Dhonda runs to me, she grabs my arm pulling me to the area reserved for us. She's had a few drinks I can tell, her eyes are closed as she slurs her words talking to the group. I use to think she was attractive until I've seen how much she drinks. Early today she spoke about how she'd wish the day would just end. She really needed a drink. Well she's surpassed that drink by a few it seems.

"What are going to have Dante," she says waving at the waitress.

"I'll just have a whiskey neat."

"Ah come on, that's a boring old man's drink," Dhonda slurs her words as she sloshes her drink in the air. The waitress nods at me before she leaves our table. When she returns she has a highball glass half full. I've never had a whiskey neat with this much in the glass.

"I like my old man's drink, it helps me think." I salute Dhonda as I take a sip from my glass.

She nods a few times before she plops down in the booth. There is no way this girl is going to make it the rest of the night. A guy I've seen around the office comes over, and shakes his head at Dhonda. She turns to look at him in that drunken way people do when they are about to say or do something stupid. She lightly taps his face as he looks disappointed as well as annoyed by her actions, but doesn't say anything.

"Dante this is my little brother David. He is my designated angel."

"Driver," David says.

"Angel you are, David," she pats him on his face again.

"I'm Dante by the way. I've seen you around the office here lately. Did you just start?" I extend my hand to the young man. He put his beer on the table to shake it.

"Yeah, my dad thought it was time to work on some of the things he doesn't want to do," he says unenthused.

"Oh okay, you're Matteson's other kid. That's cool, your dad trusts you with the important shit," I tell him to make him feel important. He side eyes me as he takes a swig of his beer.

"Its bullshit is what it is."

I laugh out loud startling Dhonda, who had fell asleep. "How many drinks have she had?"

"Four or five," David says.

"How long have you guys been here?"

It's David who laughs this time. "Less than an hour," he tells me.

I widen my eyes. I've heard things about Dhonda's drunken nights, but I never witnessed them. She will not be drinking anything else while I am here. I'm limiting myself to one. Sireen said something the resonated with me since the last time I saw her. *'But yet you sat there in the bar and continued to drink.'* Just the thought of her pisses me off. The outcome of us pisses me off. The thought of Bryant fucking her pisses me of. The sight of her is pissing me off. My drink must have gone to my heads fast. It did not. Sireen is standing at the bar, with her foot on the stool. She leans forward to speak to the bartender. He says something as he smiles at her. My resolve is slowly creeping away from me. The bartender preparing her drink is definitely flirting with her. I know he is hitting on her because the fucking idiot hits on everyone. Sireen doesn't seem like she's interested as she looks around slowly like she's inspecting the place. Her head moves slowly in my direction. I sit back in the booth with my arms spread across the length of the booth. Sireen tenses when her eyes land on mine. We stare at each other as the bartender taps the bar with her drink to get her attention. She doesn't respond to him until he leans over the bar snapping his fingers. She steps back to avoid him touching her face. My adrenaline spikes so high I don't notice the veins in my hands as I ball my fist. I flex my hand a few times to get the blood pumping again. She hands him money before she grabs her drink. It looks like Sireen likes clear liquor, it figures. Bryant drank clear liquor in college. I begin to look around to see if I can spot him. I know he's here with her, why would she come all the way to Minnesota? I honestly don't want to know. I came to relax and that's what I'm going to do. I would usually remove myself from a situation like this, I was here first, and I'm not leaving. Fuck her, and Bryant.

"I think my sister has had enough. I need to get her to the car," David says holding her hand up, then letting it fall to the table.

"You're right," I laugh. "Go ahead and pull your car to the entrance. I'll bring her out."

"Okay, thanks man. She thinks she light as a feather," he says heading to the entrance.

"C'mon little lady."

Dhonda mumbles something about her drink that she left on the table. I know she doesn't think I'm going back for it.

"You've had enough for the night little lady, let's get you

home." I say walking to the entrance.

"I think what you're doing is going to get you into some deep trouble," a soft voice from behind me says. Sireen is standing behind me with her arms folded over her chest. I glance over my shoulder, and she looks as pissed as I felt when I saw her.

"I don't give a fuck what you think."

Sireen gasps at my rudeness, I don't give a shit. She's no one to me. I wait until David opens the door so that I can leave. I lightly place Dhonda in the back seat with the seatbelt maneuvered around her body. David and I shake hands before he gets in the car. I tap the top of the car for him to pull off. Sireen is still standing in the doorway when David pulls out of the parking lot. We have a staring match before I turn to walk to my truck. I want nothing to do with her she's tainted. She and Bryant can fuck each other senseless. I hate what I've become since Sireen told me she was with Bryant. I'm bothered because I felt something for her before I knew her. Am I mental for wanting to share her sadness, and making it my own? I can't be, mental that is. No one knows how to receive sadness the way I do. I shake off the feeling of her. She's with Bryant now. I have accepted it. I start my engine, as an ill feeling comes over me. I remember I have to pass the entrance to where she stood, watching me put Dhonda in the car. Hopefully she went back to her table, and I can leave with a clear conscious.

I don't remember there being any mention of rain today. It starts to come down so hard it sounds like beating drums on my hood. As I begin to pass the entrance Sireen exits the bar. She's standing in the rain as it engulfs her small frame, while water beats the pavement around her. I can barely see her when I stop my truck in front of her. I let my window down while the rain creeps around my water resistant visor. I light a cigarette before saying anything to Sireen. I haven't smoke since I've been back, but these just happen to be in my old truck when I traded it in. I disregard the fact they're old and musty I need one to calm me down.

"You should go back in with Bryant, he'll wonder why you stood out in the rain." Sireen scowls at the mention of Bryant's name. She doesn't say anything but just looks at me. She should really try talking sometimes. I ignore her stare as I raise my window. I let out a sigh before I put my truck in drive. Dammit I shouldn't have stopped. *There goes my fucking conscious.* I put my truck back in park, and hit the locks. I stretch my body to open my door before I let my window back down.

"Get in!"

Sireen runs around the back, my truck is massively huge compared to Sireen height. I shake my head at her attempt to get in. I can't help but laugh, before I get out and help her up. The rain feels like stick pins on my skin. I picked a hell of a day to wear short sleeves without a jacket. Her waist is small in my hand as I lift her into the truck, it's like she weighs nothing. She lets out a low yelp as she holds on to my hands wrapped around her. Sireen smiles as I close the passenger side door. She fucking smiled, now my hard dick will be noticeable in these wet slacks. I think this is a bad idea. My favorite grey hat is soaked, along with my white dress shirt.

I'm driving with no determined destination. My mind tells me to ask her where should I drop her off at. I really don't care where she's going, so I head to my house. The cigarette I lit earlier has burnt out, but the scent is lingering. I will never smoke in my truck again. Sireen is looking straight ahead. She hasn't spoken a word since she got in. I'm grateful for that, I don't want her words they're temporary. I don't know what I want from her. I don't know why I opened the door, other than the fact she is standing in the rain. Her nipples are hard I can see them through her taut blouse. The bra she is wearing must be lace, due to the lack of coverage. I can even make out the brown bud of her nipple. My slacks are beginning to strain against my dick it doesn't feel good. Sireen glances over at me while I'm eyeballing her breasts. She knows, I can't help but to think this feels planned. Did Bryant tell her to get me to take her home? Is she working for him? This doesn't feel right. Bryant knows where I live. If he wanted me, he could have came to my house. Why now?

I pull up in front of my house, and shut the engine off. The rain has slowed down, so I look over at Sireen.

"Make a run for it," I ask her.

She nods, as I get out I run around to her side. She opens the door before I lower her out of the truck. "Go," I yell pointing to my house. She takes off running, splashing puddles as I follow. My walkway is longer in the rain. I feel like I ran fifty-five yards. It is probably fifty steps. I'm glad I have grips on these shoes otherwise I would have face planted.

"There goes my buzz." She wore a smile on her face before I said that. That scowl she gave me earlier is back.

"You have a problem with alcohol or something?"

"Actually, I do," she finally speaks, softly.

"You know what I have a problem with," I lean closer to her as I whisper.

"I'm sure you're going to tell me," she says licking her lips. I'm closer than I should be to her. Her lips are plump as she breaths in my air.

"Are you going to tell me?"

"You fucking other men for money," I slur out. Her reflexes are fast but mine are faster thanks to Bria. Her hand is still opened as I slide mine against hers. I link them before I cover her mouth with mine.

"Don't you ever try and slap me again," I growl ending the kiss.

Sireen nods her lowered head. Unlocking the door I push her in as it opens. She stumbles backwards, my actions catches her off guard as I move quickly to stop her from falling. I would laugh but I'm turned on by her awkwardness. The rain soaked blouse never stood a chance paired with the lace bra that is very visible, and causing my erection to painfully grow by the second. She's gasp as I rip the blouse from her skin. I lift her until we're eye to eye. Sireen wraps her legs around my waist as I push her against the wall. I've never been a kisser, but her pouty bottom lip is perfect as I suck it into my mouth. She tastes like berries, and rain as each stroke of my tongue explores hers. Releasing her mouth, I kiss her collarbone, leading a trail down her neckline while I continue to lift her until she rests her legs over my shoulders. Sireen places both hand on my head. The skirt she's wearing has risen around her waist exposing her lace panties. With my head between her legs I kiss the insides of her thighs. A soft moan escapes from her lips, and it's all I can remember thinking about. How she would sound, how would she feel? I softly kiss her sex through the lace. She's very turned on, or it rained in her panties too. Either way the lacy fabric is wet when I kiss her pussy. She tenses as I use my tongue to slide her panties to the side. Her sex is already slick from her arousal. It's taking every ounce of discipline in me not to slide inside of her, and take her hard. I won't last if I do.

"Open," I demand. She adjusts her legs over my shoulders the best she could despite her position. It's enough for me to lick her at her opening before penetrating her with my tongue. Sireen's moans are seducing me. The sound of her has increased my arousal to the point I can longer wait to have her. She's panting as I continue to use my tongue to massage her clit. I slide my tongue back to her opening using my thumb now to apply pressure to her clit. The sexiest sound I ever heard escapes her throat, when she hoarsely screams.

"I'm coming Dante! I am!"

I damn near bust one in my pants from the sound of her. Sireen squeezes my shoulder as she climaxes, her body is trembling against the wall. I lower myself so that she can easily stand. When she does I grab ahold of her ass, and lift her so that she wraps her legs around my waist again. I began leading us to my bedroom, as Sireen unbuttons my shirt. She manages to get it off my shoulders in seconds. She reaches behind me to pull the t-shirt I'm wearing over my head exposing my well-kept upper-body.

"Too many," she whispers, indicating that I have on too many shirts.

I bring my mouth to hers, kissing her so she knows how much I want this, how much I want her. My thoughts flash to her telling me how I was too late, that she had been with Bryant.

Flashes of the conversation with Bryant, enters my mind. The way

he claimed he didn't know what I was talking about when I asked

why he had fucked Sireen. The situation stops me from walking

her to the bedroom. I look into Sireen's eyes, silently we both

know why. She places her hand on my cheek, and I close my eyes

not wanting to see the truth in hers. I kiss the inside of her hand.

"Dante," she calls my name softly. "Please," she pleads with

me. It is barely audible but I heard it. I open my eyes to see the

sorrow in hers. It's the one thing in her that triggers me. I need this

from Sireen I need to drown the sorrow she holds to satisfy the

aguish I bare. It sounds sick, but it's my cure. I begin the walk

toward my bedroom again, with Sireen still holding on to me. My

bed hasn't been made up since I've left, and there's a scent of my

cologne that fills the air in the room. Sireen surprises me when she

kisses me and unwraps her legs from around me. She lowers

herself to the carpeted floor as she unbuckles my belt. No female

I've ever met took control in this way. I've always initiated them

giving me head. Sireen rubs my dick through my pants. She's

seems perplexed, I try not to laugh out at her again. She follows the bulge of my dick from the base all the way to the tip. As I look down at her she looks up. My pants are unbuttoned, and unzipped only half way as she continues to rub me through my pants. I can tell she's contemplating on whether or not she should pull it out. This is where I take control. I unzip myself a little further seeing that she's reluctant. Sireen stops me as she grabs my hand.

"Let me," her voice is still soft like she has rehearsed speaking in a low monotone. I only nod. She continues to caress my dick outside of my slacks. She finally reaches inside, grabbing a hold of my now fully erect, thick penis. She pulls is out exposing it to her completely. She pushes my slacks down so that I can step out of them. The sight of Sireen on her knees with her breast exposed, and her skirt pulled above her waist while she holds my dick in her hand is a picture that will be forever etched in my brain. My dick twitches in her hand at the sight, she looks up at me in shock. She's still holding me in her hand, but I think it's only out of courtesy because she is clearly afraid to do anything else with it.

I want to feel those pouty lips around me, but I don't want to make her uncomfortable. I leaned down to stroke her chin before I kiss her.

"You don't have to do this," I assure her. "It might be a bit too much," I tell her with a smile.

"A bit," she says questionably.

I can't help it, I laugh as she looks at me with dear stuck in the headlights eyes.

"Yeah, a little bit," I say watching her eyes dart to my lips.

"I want to," she nods.

I nod back. I kiss her again before she changes her mind. Instead of standing, I pull a chair so that we are both comfortable. I'm so much taller than her she'll need a step stool to suck my dick on her knees. The thought of that image makes me laugh, and gets me harder.

She's looking up at me as she strokes my dick in her hand. I nod at her giving her the okay. Her somber look tells me she needs direction. I sit at the edge of the chair so she doesn't have that far to reach. I rub her chin once more.

"Open."

She opens her mouth slightly so that just the tip of my dick touches her lips. She closes her eyes as she takes my entire length balls deep without gagging, shocking the pre-cum out of me. She slowly releases me as her mouth tightens like a vice grip. I can't believe what I'm feeling as she repeats her motions, but she picks up the pace. I'm holding on to the arms of the chair to refrain myself from grabbing a hold of her face, and fucking those pouty lips. The feeling of ecstasy is an understatement. Sireen softly sucks my balls and I lose my mind. My head is spinning; blood has flowed to my dick so the need to come is urgent. I can't though without feeling her. I gently pull her hair to stop her, but not before I push her as far as she can without choking. I pull her off of me, and she looks confused.

"Did I do something wrong?"

"No baby, you are so very right." I say picking her up to carry her to the bed. She seems to search my face for recognition, and I'm confused that I don't think she heard me. "You did everything so right, okay," I say to reassure her that I'm happy with the pleasure she has given to me. She smiles as I put her on the edge of the bed. I pull the skirt from her waist so that she is only wearing those lace panties. I can't help it, but I want her naked, completely. I rip the lace from her so quickly that she will bruise. I'll apologize to her in the morning for it, as I fuck her awake.

"Scoot up," I tell her. She does as I match her movement prowling towards her.

"Your so beautiful." I look into her eyes, and she rubs the stubble of my beard.

"Thank you."

We lean into each other to kiss, and it's different from the kisses before. It's longing, it feels like it's what we need. I can't help but to think what she's feeling right now at this moment. She has to want this. She stopped me from leaving. Sireen got into my truck and left the restaurant with me. Is this what she wants? I don't know why the thought of her not wanting to be here enters my mind, just like the thought of Bryant putting her up to this does. I push it all out as I continue trail kisses down her neck, nipping at her skin. I reach into the drawer beside my bed to pull out condoms. I lean away from Sireen long enough to tear the package open. I cover myself before I flick the tip of her nipple with my tongue. They are just the right size to fill my mouth. Soft moans fill my bedroom as I rest the head of my dick inside of her. I look at her for confirmation before I continue. She nods, and it's the only thing I remember before entering Sireen. She moans louder, it's such a turn on I wanted to hear her again. I withdraw from her only to glide inside of her with more force this time. The way she cries out has weakened me. It increases the sensitivity of my dick, and as tight as Sireen is I'm worried I'll come too soon.

"Harder Dante, please."

I always do as I'm asked. Without losing all control, I stroke her as hard as I think she can take. If it were left up to me, I'd drill her into the bedframe. My balls have tightened as I move inside of her. She squeezes my ass, as she screams out my name. Sireen's orgasm provokes mines. I thrust inside of her twice more before I come.

"Oh fuck! Sireen, baby!" I lay on top of her as she run the tips of her fingers across my back. It feels like heaven should feel, peaceful, and full of bliss. I can feel my seed overflowing from the condom. I knew it would, I haven't fucked anyone in a while. I can't remember the last time I shot off a good nut. I did once in Chicago, when I dreamt of Sireen's lips around my dick.

"Are you okay," I ask.

Sireen nudges me so that she can move from under me. I don't want to move, but I can imagine how uncomfortable my body weight is on hers. I brush strands of her hair away from her face. She smiles and kisses my hand, her soft lips lingers on the inside of my hand.

"Sireen, baby, are you okay?" She briefly glances at my lips then back at me.

"I am, thank you for asking. Sireen caresses her thumb over

my lips.

"Are you sure I didn't hurt you,"

"It was a pleasurable pain," she says still rubbing the pad of her thumb over my lips. I kiss the tip of her thumb, and pull her close to me as I rollover onto my back. She changes her position so that she is facing me. I can stare into her brown eyes forever, and I will if she gives me a chance.

"Don't move."

"Okay," she says pulling the sheets above her waist. When I return from disposing the condom Sireen is laying on her stomach, only half her body is covered. Her perfectly round ass print is exposed through the sheet. The sight alone gets me hard. She looks at me with shock in her eyes, as my dick becomes erect. Normally I'd be embarrassed by my reaction to a woman, but somehow I think she's appreciative of the recovery time.

"So soon," she says eyeing my erection.

"Not soon enough."

I grab another condom from the drawer, and kneel over her

on the bed. Sireen begins to turn over. I place my free hand on her ass to stop her.

"Don't," I lean over her shoulder to whisper in her ear. I snatch the sheet that is between us, off, exposing her naked body. Her body tells a story, she has tattoos in random places. The one that catches my eye is the one that wraps around the side of her waist. I didn't notice it earlier, because I was pre-occupied with the rest of her. It's a banner design of words. I'll inspect it later, right now her ass is all I can think about. I roll the condom as far as it goes. It's like using a half sandwich baggie for a whole sandwich. I can't help that my dick is bigger than the largest condoms I could find. I lick my thumb before I test the waters. Sireen tenses up when I circle the rim of her ass with my thumb.

"Dante. Please, not there," her soft voice pleads with me.

"Shhh, I won't baby. Just relax." I kiss her on the ass before I spread her cheeks apart. Sireen lets out a hoarse moan as kiss her between her ass cheeks. She moans louder than she had, as I lick her pussy from behind. The way her body is responding I know she's ready. It's such a fucking turn to know I do this to her. I can get off on just her reaction alone. I continue to suck on her clit, as her orgasm hits her hard. Her body is trembling harder than before, so much that I want to feel her sex contract around my dick. I quickly slide inside of her as she climaxes. I grab the headboard with both my hands for leverage, and slam into her, again. She lets out a cry, as I fuck her from behind. I lift her ass for deeper penetration, the more of me she feels; the more she knows how serious I am about pleasing her. Sireen grabs the sheets with both hands as she calls out to me. It's low, but I know she's saying my name.

My orgasm is close, as I look down at Sireen's body. Beads of sweat coats her, making strands of her wavy hair stick to her back. I pull her up, so that she's fully kneeling with her back to my front. The angle makes me thrust harder into her. I pull her hair away from her shoulder with one hand splaying the other around her neck. Her lips are what did it for me. They've swollen from giving me head earlier. She whispers into my mouth as I kiss them.

"You feel so good inside me Dante,"

Those simple words are what tighten my balls this time. I lost any resolve in thinking. Thinking I would last longer, and pound into her until my body jerks into exhaustion. "Shit!" I say collapsing on top of her. "I'm sorry Sireen, baby. I couldn't hold it in any longer."

She cups my face from behind, her fingertips dancing at the apex of my ear. Sireen hunches her shoulders forcing me to peel my body from hers. She rolls onto her back exposing her breast. I can't help myself I lower my head to suck her nipple into my mouth. Sireen hums as I circle her bud with the tip of my tongue.

"You're going to get me all wet again," she says half laughing.

"That's the point, I want to make sure you stay ready for me," I say releasing her from my mouth.

"For you?" A questioning stare crosses her face.

"For only me," I say sternly so that she knows I'm serious. I've had a taste of her now. The want, the need to have her again is unmistakably inevitable.

Sireen looks away. I cup her chin to force her to look at me. Within a slow blink of her eyes a rush of trepidation hits her, and I can see the panic on her face.

"I shouldn't have come here," she says reaching for the sheets to try and cover herself.

"What changed from the time I ripped your blouse off until the time I just made you come in my mouth? Because I'm pretty sure you're the same person whom jumped in front of my truck in the pouring rain. What the fuck did you think was going to happen? There's no rainbows and sunshine after the rain on this side of town Sireen, only dark clouds, and nights over here. If you're lucky, you'll see a star or two." I push up, away from her trying to distance myself from her regrets. She sinks down into the sheets as if she's scared. Even though I wasn't easy on her from the time she got in my truck tonight up until now, it still pains me to see her afraid. I reach for her, but she doesn't budge from the spot she's covering herself in.

"Sireen, please, come here."

She's hesitant before rises to her knees, still covering her body as she shuffles the sheets between her legs. She crossed the bed to me, stopping to pull more of the sheet that follows her.

"I'm sorry. I didn't—,"

She leans forward to kiss me silent. It is a kiss to begin another session of mind altering fucking, followed by intense lovemaking. She opened up and showed me what I don't think I can't live without. Bryant can go to hell. I have everything I need now. I'm set for life, and Sireen will be a part of it. He can never have her again.

CHAPTER 8

THE NEXT MORNING

Bryant

I tried to stay calm in this situation, but I couldn't sit back and do nothing. Dante can't come to claim what's mine for his, and expect me to not come for him. He's been silent all of this time with this information. When his mother died, I knew I would be free from the secrets she carried, and buried with her. I'm still in the dark about how Dante found out about the payments. The son of a bitch did, he came for what he thinks is his. I thought I could let it go after the money was wired, but I thought about what he said to me over the phone. It wasn't until I got back to Minnesota I understood. I saw how he looked at Sireen in the lobby of the hotel. His body language changed in the restaurant when we stopped at his table. Dante had a murderous look on his face when he saw me with her. I'm sure he wanted to kill me when I pulled

Sireen close to me before we walked away. He thinks I fucked her maybe I should after what I have planned goes down. It'll be the sweetest revenge, it's not like we've haven't fucked the same female before.

I asked Sireen to come to Minnesota to seduce Dante. I gave her two days to get it done in return I'll pay her when she delivers his checkbook. She only wanted enough money to pay for a surgery, I didn't care to ask because she's Bria's employee not mine. I try to not get involved with anyone's personal business. It opens a door, a door to care, and I don't. The only thing I care about theses days is my money. It only takes one check to pay myself back what Dante took from me. She told me it would be better to take the entire checkbook, so it looks like he lost it. One check would be too suspicious and he'd know exactly who had taken it from him. It's not about the money, it's because Dante is an arrogant bastard child who thinks he can come and take a part of what I built. He'll pay for it though.

The sun is barely rising, and my doorbell rings. I pull myself out of bed slowly trying to ignore the pain I've been in for the past few days. I've been pushing my body to the extreme to work off the stress this has caused me. Fifty million dollars of my own money is a hard pill to swallow when I just invested twice as much, and haven't seen a return on it yet. I peek out of the small window on my door to see the face of what I will look like at forty-seven. My Dad, and I haven't spoken since he divorced my mother. I began to walk away to leave his cheating ass on the step, but he beats on the door.

"Son, I know you're in there, you might as well let me in."

I open the door, pulling it with enough force that it bounces off the wall as it flies open. I don't bother seeing him in. I walk away to grab a t-shirt. I glance back at my dad letting himself in, inspecting the wall as he closes the door.

"Good to see you too, son."

They way he says it fuels the fire inside of me knowing that I'm not his only son. I pull a shirt over my head angrily.

"Are you sure," I ask sarcastically.

"Sure of what, being good to see you?"

"No, being your son."

He looks confused, so I help him out.

"So Charlotte wasn't the only woman you cheated on my mom with, was she?"

He's running his hands through his hair nervously.

"Look, son, that's not what I came here to tell you about, but since it seems like this is what your sudden dislike for me is about, I'll tell you. There were women before I married your mother. Women she never knew about, or I cared to tell her about because I ended things with them when we married. I want us to get past this."

"Bullshit, you tried to cover it up," I yelled.

"I didn't. Everything was okay until Bev got sick. I wanted to help her with her hospital bills."

"She had a husband, and that wasn't until later," I grit through my teeth.

"He died son," he says with sadness.

"I don't care, so did she," I say walking into my kitchen. I need a drink, but it's too damn early.

"I know son," he says following me.

"Do you! Do you know she has a son?"

"I do."

"Do you now, and do you know I fixed your fuck up? Do you know she came to me about a will you gave her, in the event you died? It stated that her son would have received half of your company. The company you let die because of your bad decisions. The company you withdrew millions from keeping your whores happy, and my mother sitting at home waiting for you. You know how I know she waited for you? I was there with her. I brought my company back from the dead," I pound my fist on my chest as I continue to tell my father to go fuck himself. "Me, I did what you failed at doing. Me, I did that. Then you go and give that woman's son half of a company I resuscitated. I paid her to go away, and I took that will and burnt it in mom's fireplace."

"You did what?"

"Are you losing your hearing old man? I burnt that fucking will in mom's fireplace."

"You selfish son of a bitch, that wasn't for you to decide. You should want someone to work beside you after I'm gone."

"Nah, I'm good."

"You have incriminated yourself admitting this to me."

I ignore his comment, I'm sure he knows I'm aware of what I did.

"You should go, I have a long day at the office tomorrow. Someone has to make rational decisions. I guess we know it won't be you."

"Bryant, don't get beside yourself. I still own a fair share of my company, any thing that you do has to come through me."

"Dad, we voted you out months ago, you're too damn busy chasing skirts to notice. Did you think nothing was going on all this time? I make action moves. How do you think you got moved right out the door?"

My father has never been strict. He came and went as he

pleased in both my mother, and my life. He taught me the business the nice way. I learned the business the cutthroat way through his actions. We could have been great together.

"What do you mean, I'm voted out? I just signed paperwork for the hotel stock investments."

"You did," I pause before I break it to him. He needs to know exactly what he signed. "You also signed your percentage of the company over to me." I shrug. "You've always taught me to read every piece of document that requires a signature. Good advice, dad." My father has never raised his hand to me, but at this moment the anger on his face says he just may change his parenting views.

"You will reap what you sow, Bryant. If you live long enough."

"Is that a threat, dad," I ask mocking him.

"No Bryant, you'll do it to yourself," my dad says impassively. He turns his back and begins to walk out.

"You were good at making things disappear, dad. Company

money, yourself. I didn't learn that from you, because motherfuckers keep coming back when I try and get rid of them."

"That's funny son. You know that saying, what's in the dark shall come to light? You'll never know who's lurking in the dark holding the switch," he says with his back still to me. He walks out of my kitchen without saying goodbye. There's a faint sound of voices, followed by the door closing. I leave my kitchen to see what the hell my dad is saying. It's not what it's who. Sireen stands silently in my living room wearing oversized sweatpants, and a t-shirt that hangs from under her jacket.

"What are you doing here?" She stares at me like she didn't understand.

"Sireen, why are you here?"

Sireen reaches into her jacket pocket, removing what looks like a checkbook. I can't believe she managed to boost Dante's checkbook out of his house. I knew he was easy, but this was too easy. I hold out my hand for her to give it to me, but she doesn't. She shakes her head.

"Pay me first," she says holding the checkbook against her chest. Every fucking body has their hand out. I should have known I couldn't just get something for nothing.

"Not so fast, how do I know that what you are holding has checks in it?"

She opens it, holding up the pocketbook with what looks like a few checks have been torn out.

"It was in his coat pocket, so it's recent. Why do you need his checkbook anyway?

"It's business sweetheart," I tell her stepping closer with my hand extended. I can see the reluctance in her stare.

"Bryant, where's my money?"

"Fine, just a minute," I leave to get her a check for the amount we agreed about, when I return she's gone. She fucking left with Dante's checkbook.

"Dammit! It's too fucking early for this!"

Within The Hour

Dante

The warmth I once felt from Sireen's body has now diminished. I roll over to pull her perfectly small body close to me, but there is a cold space where her body once laid. Instantly I'm pissed off, because I know she's gone. If she were in the bathroom, her side of the bed should still be warm. She came so many times last night there's no way my bed should be cold and stale from the aftermath of a warm body. I sit up to look around my room, crucifying myself for falling asleep. I haven't slept that hard in months. It was long overdue, and I regret every minute of it. I planned on waking her up with my dick growing inside her. Instead I'm sitting here thinking about it. We fucked and made love all over this room last night, why would she leave without telling me. What is she afraid of? A small part of me knew she would run. She had regrets after our second round. A small part of me also wanted to wake up next to her this morning.

"Dammit, Sireen!" I push my knuckles into the mattress to

avoid punch it.

My doorbell surprises me when it chimes. I remember when I installed it I couldn't hear the test ring the instructions guided me through. I pulled on shorts just in case this isn't Sireen who didn't lock herself out. I've never been an underwear type of guy, but she should know that now. I don't bother looking through the small opening on my door, I pull it open ready to give Sireen a physical tongue lashing for not waking me up with a blow job like we agreed upon last night. Only it isn't Sireen on the other side of the door. The older guy turns around with a shocked look on his face. He looks so familiar, but I don't place him right away.

"Hi, can I help you," I ask holding on to the door.

He doesn't say anything right away, but he just stares at me. The way he stands, the way he holds his hands in his pockets resembles someone. I know I've seen this guy around town, but it's not coming to me. His stare is even familiar. He looks like... *Bryant.* It hits me like a fucking freight truck, it rocks me so hard I stumble back. Reaching out trying to close the door, but I fail miserably.

"You look just like your mother," he says with a smile like Bryant's and my own.

"I'm Mr. Morg—,"

"I know who the fuck you are," I say harshly.

"You, and your brother have that temper in common,"

"I'm nothing like his selfish ass, and I'm nothing like your weak, cowardly ass. How the fuck dare you come to my mother's house, my house," I spat.

He steps forward, right at the threshold of my living room.

"I was fine never knowing you. You are not welcomed here, or anywhere I am." All the pain I've felt over the years from losing my parents, never knowing the real father Bryant, and I share overwhelmed me. The anxiety that I am experiencing has risen dangerously high. I begin to breathe erratically as I have double over trying to calm myself.

"Son are you okay," Mr. Morgan, ask me placing his hand on my shoulder.

"Don't fucking touch me," I say violently moving my

shoulder from under his hand.

"I only want to help Dante."

I glance up at him. I've lost my words, and I swear all I see is red. I could kill him right now in this very house. I can barely lift my arm, as my chest constricts with pain. I point behind him indicating he should leave.

"Son, you don't look good," he says concerned. His face displays worry, as he pulls out his cell phone.

"Leave," is all I manage to say. I feel light headed as I try looking up. In the distance I can see a car at the curb. I can't make out who is in the back seat, and I don't have to. I know its Sireen. She came back to me. A feeling of satisfaction fills me to know she's back. Everything becomes blurry, just like the car pulling away with Sireen in it.

"Siree—," I try calling out, falling to the ground.

"Son, I've called the ambulance. Just hold on," is all I heard before I blacked out.

CHAPTER 9

TWO HOURS LATER

Dante

I wake up on a hard slate of a mattress with tubes attached to everything on my body that has a hole, except my mouth. The loneliest feeling is to open your eyes and have no one. A doctor comes in with a clipboard.

"Mr. Morgan?"

"No, it Williams. I'm not a Morgan," my response came off harsher than I meant it to be.

"Okay, Mr. Williams, you've had what is called heart palpitations. You had a severe panic attack, which caused your heart to beat at a rapid rate. The pain in your chest is one of the symptoms, and the issue we were mostly concerned about. I want you to follow up with your doctor next week to run a few precautionary tests."

"What kind of precautionary test," I ask.

"Precautionary," Bryant sarcastically says from behind the doctor.

"Are you family," the doctor asks Bryant.

"Unfortunately."

"Well, I'll let you visit with him for few minutes. Try not to get upset," the doctor says as he leaves the room.

"Why are you here?"

Bryant's lips are turned down, as he shakes his head. "I'm not here for you, I'm making sure Sireen wasn't here."

"No she's not. You can be gone too."

"Take it easy, you heard what the doctor said, brother," Bryant says indirectly.

I want nothing to do with Bryant, his father or Sireen. When I'm able to leave the hospital I'm going on a much needed vacation.

"You'll never be a brother of mine, get the fuck out and go find who you're looking for."

"What are you saying, I'm your only brother," he laughs at his own joke.

"Bryant if you don't leave I swear I'll call that Waters chick, and drop the whole fucking story in her lap."

That gets his attention. Bryant's grinds his teeth as he contemplates whether or not I'll do it. He doesn't want to test me he knows what I'm capable of. Bryant's phone rings, and he taps the screen to answer.

"Hold on," he tells the person on the other end. "Tell Sireen to return what she came to Minnesota to get," he says to me before continuing his phone call as he leaves the room.

The next day the hospital releases me with strict instructions. I'm supposed to avoid stressful situations. If I find myself in them I am to keep my cool. I can't drink caffeine, which is fine because I only drink bourbon, another fucking thing I have to avoid. *Doctor's order.* When I get home there's a small padded envelope on my floor from where the mail carrier slid it into the slot. It has no postage on it, only my first name is written in black ink. There is no return address on the envelope. These little details cause me to be apprehensive when opening it. It's my checkbook with a folded piece of paper sticking out of it. It's a hand written letter. The pit of my stomach is in knots knowing that this letter is from Sireen. I scan the letter quickly to confirm what I know. Right at the very end of the letter her love signature stands out like carnations in a rose garden. It's rare. Next to it there's a date, dated for tomorrow at noon. I scan the letter again to see what the date and time are associated with. It's a little café she wants me to meet her at. I fold the letter up not bothering to read it. I shove it into the pocket of my jacket not caring what she wrote in the letter. I'll wait until tomorrow to speak to Sireen. The letter is the last fucking thing on my mind. The fact that it is joined with my checkbook has me confused. Why had she taken it?

THE NEXT DAY

Dante

The café I'm meeting Sireen at is very secluded. I wonder why did she choose this particular café? I've been living in Minnesota all my life there's no way I would have found this place without trying. I double-check the address again before I go in. "1820 3rd Ave," I say to no one. I'm not sure how long Sireen's been in Minnesota, but I'm sure it wasn't long enough to find this place. I order a non-caffeinated tea with a bagel just to hold me over until I find something I really want to eat. The café sits on an angle, which intersects with three other corners. The angle provides a wide view because it sits behind the three points that makes the corner. I find a seat away from the door, but in plain view of the main street to the café. Glancing at the Greek styled clock above the window, Sireen is late. I'm not surprised she has a lot of explaining to do. She can't prolong the inevitable though. The longer she takes to get here the harder it becomes for her to tell me about why she left, or anything else she's done since I met her.

An hour has passed, and Sireen hasn't showed up. I ignore the fact the barista's have offered me free food out of pity. They know I've been stood up, but I haven't accepted it yet. My stomach hurts from the stress I've encountered in the last few hours of sitting here. I pull out the letter I refused to read last night, because deep down I wanted this to be real. I wanted to come here to see Sireen, listen to her reason behind taking my checks, fucking me, then leaving. I knew when I walked into this café I didn't care why she did those things. I wanted her anyway. The fact that Bryant had her first doesn't bother me as much now that I've been with her in ways I know Bryant hasn't. I got in Sireen's head last night, I felt the ways she surrender her body to me. The way she held on to me as she climaxed. Bryant didn't do that, I did. I stare at the letter before unfolding it. It's not what I want to do but I read it anyway.

-Dante,

The moment you held on to me in the elevator that night I knew you were someone special. That night, that moment, your arms were my protection. You shielded me from the cruel reality that I had to go home to. Ironically your presence brought the sweetest serene to my soul. All the times we kept crossing paths I thought it must be fate. I left you a piece of me in the elevator every time the doors closed. It was torture to leave a place I knew that was meant for me. My life isn't simple, and I took advantage of a situation that presented itself to be beneficial to me. I knew leaving the restaurant with you was wrong, because it was under false pretenses. I want to apologize to you in person if you allow me to. There are things in my life that I'm afraid to admit to anyone, but not to you. I felt every part of you last night, and yet, still I think there is more. You showed me that I'm capable of being wanted, maybe even loved. I'll understand if you don't show up, but I want you to know why I did the things I did. Dante, I never meant to hurt you, and yet I sit here writing this letter to you to ask you for your forgiveness. I promise I'll explain everything at the little café on the corner, tomorrow at noon. Just please be there.

1830 3rd Ave. S.

With Love,

Serene Sireen

I don't know why, but I'm pissed off. Maybe it's because I knew I was right about her not actually showing up. I begin to think of all the shit I've been through these past weeks. I keep reverting back to the things Bryant said, 'Tell Sireen to return what she came to Minnesota to get.' What the fuck did she come here to get that she has to return? The light bulb goes off in my head. She took my fucking checkbook. I pull it from the inside of my pocket, fingering through the rectangle pages. The last check is missing, and immediately it all comes together. "Fucking Bryant," I yell as I spring up from my chair, knocking over the chair I was sitting in. I sprint out to my truck holding on to the last piece of Sireen. I don't care to get caught in the afternoon traffic. I drive down Third Avenue, going south as fast as my truck can go without breaking the speed limit. All I can think is how I am going to beat the hell out of Bryant for putting Sireen up to this. As I come to a stop sign in the residential area, a female exits a small café' on the corner. I stare at the piece of paper I forgot I had balled up in my hand. The address is the same as the café I was sitting in for over three hours waiting for Sireen. The address on the window has an S for south after it, just like Sireen wrote in her letter. I hadn't taken the time to notice it when I entered it in my navigation system. All this time I thought Sireen stood me up, and it was me who was in the wrong place. I'm such a fucking idiot. A car horn blows for me to cross the intersection. Just as I do, she walks out of the café'. Sireen, walks out of the café I am supposed to be at. I blow my horn to get her attention, but she doesn't notice me. The café is on the opposite side of the street, so it's hard to get to her from my truck. I blow my horn a few more times, but she continues to look at her phone. I doubled park my truck to get across the street to her. Impatient drivers yell out there windows for me to move. I speed down the street meaning to U-turn, but there is no room. I have to catch up to her. I don't know why she didn't hear my horn, its massive in sound. I'm shocked it didn't scare her. Circling the block, I get caught in traffic of residents leaving their parking garages.

"Shit," I grunt out.

I park in an alley and decide to run the rest of the way. As I round the corner the café sits across the street, Sireen is standing outside. I call out to her, but she doesn't look up. I think she's wearing headphones, but it doesn't appear that way. I call her name again, and this time she looks up but in the direction of a car. She must have requested a taxi, but she still hasn't noticed me. Cars are zipping pass as I try to cross the street. Before she gets in she looks back as I yell her name. It is no use she doesn't hear me, and I stand there watching my life drive away in a taxi. The beat of my heart has slowed, maybe because it just rode off with Sireen.

As I walk back to my truck I contemplate on chasing the car she left in. I have second thoughts when I believe she might be on her way to my house. Excitement races through me as I drive home, but soon diminishes when I pull up.

"She's not here," I say aloud.

As I go in, Bryant pulls up. The amount of anger I feel right now should be illegal. I stand with both feet apart, with my hands balled into fist. "What the fuck do you want, cause I'm pretty sure it ain't here," I say roughly.

He looks like he's as pissed as I am as he walks up to me. I push Bryant before he gets any closer.

"D! I'm not here to fucking fight you," he spits. "As much as I want you to burn in hell for the bullshit you pulled with Eve Waters, I'm here to tell you about Sireen." My body stills at the mention of her name. Bryant runs his hand through his hair.

"Look, I hired her to steal your checks, but the bitch ran off with all of them."

I don't let Bryant know that she returned them, because I want to know what he offered her.

"She came to me with them, and I left the room to—," Bryant pauses mid-sentence. He looks bewildered at first, as his thoughts begin to come together. He looks up at me.

"What," I ask with bot arms extended.

"She played us," he said as a matter of fact. *No she played you.*

"She said she needed money for some kind of surgery."

"What kind of surgery?"

"I don't fucking, know. I didn't give a shit about that. I just needed her to steal your checks so I can get my money back."

That's not happening.

"So let me get this straight, you paid her to steal from me so you could steal from me too? Only she stole what you paid her to steal from me, from you. That's some epic shit right there Bryant. Stupid, epic, asshole shit!"

Bryant glares at me before he starts to laugh. "She played us," he says, again.

She played you. I'm definitely not telling Bryant anything about Sireen. He can't be trusted as long I have this money, and I'm not giving it up.

"Looks that way, I'll cancel those checks. No one will get anything."

"If she hasn't already," he says rubbing his chin.

"Maybe, but she has no clue what I have. That information is only available to me, you, and the bank," I say pointing between Bryant and me.

"I don't believe that, what other way than flashing money did you get her into your bed," he asks bluntly.

"Definitely not the way you got her in yours," I say coldly.

"You think I fucked her, is that why you didn't back off? Are you having flashbacks from all the times I charmed the females from under you. Well you hadn't got that far with them for them to be under you. I treated Sireen, just like I treated Bria all those years ago," he says cynically.

Flashes of red are all I see before I tackle Bryant to the ground. One thing Bryant, and I don't have in common is left hooks. I bore my knuckles into him as he lies on the ground with blood spewing from his nose. It isn't until one of my neighbors pulls me off of him that I realized what I've done. Bryant body is lifeless as he lies in my driveway. A few seconds pass before I here sirens echoing through the streets. When the ambulance arrives Bryant's face is filled with blood, mostly his even though I bust my knuckles across his jaw. I've never beaten anyone unconscious; I've never had a temper. The EMT's waves a bottle of smelling salt under Bryant's nose. He regains consciousness. Bryant waves his hand for me to come to him. I walk closer so that I can hear him.

"I didn't fuck her. Like I said, she played us." He lifts his arm as far as the restraints allow him, and extends his thumb. "Nice left hook, I won't tell dad," he says sardonically. Bryant is lifted into the ambulance. The sirens are activated as they pull out of my driveway.

Two weeks has passed, I haven't heard anything from Bryant since I disfigured his face. I was certain that he'd have me arrested for assault. I thought about paying him a visit, but I changed my mind as soon as the thought entered it. He's a grown ass man, who can take an ass kicking every once in a while. Brother or not, I don't like him. I probably never will. The father we share is all we have. I don't care to know either of them more than I already do. He confessed that he hadn't slept with Sireen, but I don't care about that either. Sireen is a ghost to me. Every time she's in my thoughts a chill comes over me. I've tried not to hate her, but I'm currently on my way to the bank to verify a check I did not write. Knowing Sireen had my checks, I'm sure she's the person who wrote it.

When I enter the bank I let the personal banker know whom I'm here to see. I'm escorted in the secure area of the bank, not a bullpen separated by partitions. This has to be more serious than I thought. *How much did she take?*

"Hi Mr. Williams, I'm Steve Holmes. I am the senior manager of the fraud department for the bank. I've brought you here to confirm some suspicious activity on your account."

"Okay," I simply reply. The manager looks at me with concern.

"Mr Williams, did you write any checks lately?"

"No."

"Someone did," he pulls out a copy of the check, and slides

it across the table. Everything on the check is blurred out, except the signature. I take a seat to inspect it. I can tell it's Sireen's handwriting, but I don't tell Steve that.

"No, this isn't me," I tell him.

"Do you know who it is? If you don't know, we have tracked down the hospital it is written to, what it is for, and the amount it is for. It seemed odd because none of your other checks were written before this one. That's what brought it to our attention, and the amount," he says as a matter of factly.

"How much?"

The manager's eyes widen, "I know you have quite a bit of money Mr. Williams, but one hundred thousand dollars is not a small sum to miss. Did your checks get stolen? We can investigate anyone who you may think that could have done this. With the all of the Hippa laws we can't obtain 'the who,' information from the hospital," he uses air quotes. "Until we go forward with a full investigation."

I can feel all of the blood leaving my face. I can't believe

Sireen stole a hundred thousand from me. I'm not revengeful, but I want her to pay for this. The money means nothing, but I can't let her get away with it. The pussy was great, but not a hundred k great. I should have planted my seed in her if I knew she would pull this shit. We cold have had little golden babies and shit for a hundred k.

"Mr. Williams, are you okay?"

"Fuck no, I'm not. What do I have to do to find out who did this," I ask pretending like I don't already know.

"Well you have to sign these papers that state you want to go forward with a full investigation, and prosecution upon the findings of said investigation." He slides a few sheets of papers to me with instructions on where to sign. I sign all three sheets before I slide them back to him.

"Okay, we're all set Mr. Williams. We'll contact you when we have a name, as well as the actions that follow. Do you have any questions," he asks as he shakes my hand. I didn't want to know what kind of surgery she had, or whether or not it was for her at all. She seems thoughtful that way. I didn't want to do any of this I wanted let Sireen off without getting her into any trouble. The more I think about it, the more it pisses me off that she might be one of those females who feels she needs cosmetic surgery to get ahead in life. If that's the case, whatever she bought with my money I want it back. Ass. Boobs. Lips. All of it, I want it back. The thought of her lips wrapped around my dick is not something I should be thinking about at the moment. I have to know though. It'll eat at me forever.

"You said you've tracked down the hospital and what it's for?"

"We did, lets see," he says thumbing through the stack of papers. "Yes, it was at University of Chicago for a cochlear implant surgery," he says like I'm aware what the hell that is. I draw my eyebrows together, confused at what he said.

"A what?"

"Whoever that wrote this check paid for implants."

"Implants," I repeated the manager's words. "What kind of

implants?"

I knew she was that type female, not happy with what God gave her.

"Uhhh, hearing implants," the manager confirms.

"Hearing implant," I ask, repeating what the manager says again.

"Yes, whoever wrote this check was deaf."

There's a brief moment of silence between the bank manager and myself before I comprehend. Every moment with Sireen dawns on me.

"Sireen's, deaf…"

The End

Acknowledgements

Hi everyone!

I want to say thank you to all the readers, bloggers, and authors who have supported me. Whether it was a share, a like, or word of mouth you are appreciated. To the planners, and hosts thank you for supporting me as well. Remember a world without books, is a like a world, without...

~OY

About the Author

O.Y. Flemming is a Chicagoan who lives... Yes, lives her city. Chicago is partly why she writes. The city gives her stories life as she incorporates her creativity into each novel.

Her love for books started at an early age, but as an adult she was re-introduced to reading again and found a love for storytelling. Her style of writing is filled with intriguing storylines, and classy acts of sexiness where even an open book has hidden messages.

In O.Y.'s downtime she loves blending different coffee together creating the perfect coffee hybrid. When she's not sleeping; procrastinating; or obsessing over cars, she's reading.

O.Y. loves to create a thrilling story as she writes. She hopes to try her hand in young adult fiction to be considered for high school reading curriculum.

O.Y. is an open book, torn pages kinda author. You want to know what that's all about? Ask her.

oyflemming@gmail.com

Like me on Facebook https
@oyflemmingauthor

Follow me on IG:
@oyflemmingauthor

twitter.com/ojhoana
@Ojhoana

Made in the USA
Columbia, SC
06 October 2022

68609352R00107